Nicholas and Alex know one thing for sure: they want to spend their lives together, and now that they're engaged, they can start planning their big day to make that happen. The only hitch? Both of them have very different ideas on what that means.

Nicholas has been all about a grand wedding since he was a teen, carefully planning every detail from floral arrangements to the perfect cake. He has big dreams and a bigger budget to make it happen. But Alex? Despite finding the love of his life, he's still a little jaded, and he'd rather elope at the local courthouse, keeping the start of their married life low-key.

Can they set aside their different ideas on their big wedding and compromise to make it the wedding of their dreams, or will a major tragedy be the final blow after they struggle to see eye-to-eye?

I0591365

THIS VOW

This Love, Book Two

J.R. Hart

A NineStar Press Publication

www.ninestarpress.com

This Vow

Printed in the USA

ISBN: 978-1-64890-294-9

First Edition, May, 2021

Also available in eBook, ISBN: 978-1-64890-293-2

CONTENT WARNING:
This book contains sexually explicit material which is only suitable for mature readers, references to a dead parent, homophobia, and trauma (fire).

To Gram, whose love of reading sparked mine.

Author's Note

I began writing *This Vow* in November 2019, long before COVID-19 was a reality in our world. In this book, which does deal with themes of illness, as well as many events and gatherings, you won't see any mentions of masks, social distancing, or the new reality we all face together. As an author, I had to look at this manuscript and decide a way forward: did I want to edit this to include the pandemic we are all facing, or leave it the way it was written, in hopes that it offered a sense of escape from the new life we live? During the editing process, mentions of parties and hugging made me cringe, but I wanted to share this story in the spirit it was written.

While future series and books I write may mention the pandemic in some way, this series will continue in the vein it was started: in a world without a global pandemic. Consider the world of *This Christmas*, *This Vow*, and the subsequent books an alternate reality where COVID-19 was not on our radar.

Prologue

"Nicholas, there's a fire, in the kitchen! We have to go!"

Bleary-eyed from sleep, Nicholas didn't grasp what Alex was saying. "Fire?" He didn't comprehend the box of recipes in his hand, why Alex was shoving them at him frantically. Drowsiness from cold medication and the deep sleepfulness of his nap didn't help matters, a slur of loud, blaring alarms sounding in his mind as he tried to pay attention to what Alex was telling him.

"In the kitchen! We have to get out of here, Nicholas. Carry the recipes! Let's *go!*" Alex insisted.

Fire? His brain repeated the word. Fire. *Fire!* Oh gosh. He glanced around him, trying to take stock of what they might be able to save. "Okay, um…" They had to get their things, important memories and items from around the apartment. Why was Alex in the bedroom instead of grabbing their photos off the walls and the box of notes they'd written each other early in their relationship out of the closet?

"Nicholas, we don't have time to get stuff. It's spreading too fast. We have to go." Nicholas followed Alex's eyeline up to the smoke entering the bedroom, watching as he raced toward the living room, and the urgency finally started to click into place. A fire. An *actual* fire. Not the hypothetical "what three items would you save in a fire?" kind of situation, but a real-life, honest-to-God fire. "Oh no." Stumbling out of the bedroom and closing the door out of habit, he could see the flames now, the bright-orange flickers of light in the kitchen. He started toward the source of it, the location of most of his prized possessions, but Alex yanked him back by the arm.

"Crawl!" Alex urged him. "We have to crawl over there." Alex ducked down, tugging his shirt up to cover his mouth and nose. Nicholas followed suit, grasping the recipe box and moving ahead, trying to get to the door and open it while Alex scanned the room. Halfway there, the half wall dividing the kitchen from the entryway shook with a loud bang. Something in the kitchen exploded. "Oh my God!" Alex yelped.

"What was that?" Nicholas assumed the explosion came from some pressurized can like cooking spray, or the bottle of their favorite whiskey they enjoyed on poker nights with the girls. His brain lagged behind the urgency of the situation, focused on the things being consumed by the fire creeping closer.

"I don't know!" Alex's words jarred him back into the moment. "Let's go to the balcony," he pleaded. The fire escape there hadn't worked in years, but Nicholas agreed that outside, regardless of a way down, was the safer bet. If anything, they could breathe fresh air out there instead of toxic smoke in their apartment.

Alex crawled in the other direction and Nicholas followed, watching Alex slide the glass door open and let him through. Both of them stood and closed the door to seal the blaze behind them. "Now what?"

If the fire got any closer, Nicholas figured the heat could shatter the glass. Was it the movie *Backdraft* that happened in? He didn't know why his mind focused on Hollywood hypotheticals instead of on the reality of what was happening to his home, his life. Maybe because his brain was on a delay, hadn't fully registered the intensity of the situation.

Alex pushed their mostly dead succulents in front of the door and nestled Nicholas against the railing of the balcony that didn't line up with the glass, putting them out of harm's way. He must have been thinking the same thing about the glass shattering. "Call 9-1-1," Nicholas told Alex. Drilled into his head from countless school fire safety classes, he didn't have to even think. But then the reality of what was happening hit him all over again. A lot of their beloved belongings continued to burn. Maybe they had time... "We forgot—"

"Nicholas, we can't go back in," Alex reminded him. "Whatever we've forgotten, it's not important."

Right. Good enough. Getting out alive had to be good enough. Nicholas nodded, tearing up as Alex pulled his phone out of his pocket.

"What are you doing?"

"Telling Jade to pull the building fire alarm," he said. Their own smoke alarm only sounded in their apartment, barely loud enough for the neighboring apartments to hear. This was a good thing when the alarm sounded for minor problems, like grease popping around eggs, but not a great feature when it came to a real fire. Then, Alex's voice switched to no-nonsense mode as he called 9-1-1, waiting till he was connected and then explaining the fire to the dispatcher.

Nicholas could hear the fire alarms blaring clearly now. Jade must have done as he asked. From the balcony, Nicholas saw the edges of the flames licking at the picture they'd hung on the wall after their engagement. He turned away. He couldn't bear to look at the fire taking away everything they owned, every precious memory they'd shared in the apartment. Looking down at the ground, he spotted people filtering out of the front doors of the building, staring up to them on the balcony above. "What the heck happened?"

"I was trying to make you soup," Alex admitted, followed by, "I'm so sorry."

The guilt in his voice was palpable, breaking Nicholas's heart. "Baby, it's all right." As the trucks backed up, ladders extending, Alex cried against him, his free arm around him. Alex sobbed harder than Nicholas had ever seen him cry.

"I'm so sorry," he repeated and then he turned toward the ladder, heading down with Nicholas climbing after him, cradling the recipes in his arm. He listened to the sound of the crackle through the sliding glass door as the contents of their lives went up in smoke.

Chapter One

A Summer Cold

Two weeks earlier

Even with a pillow covering his ears to block out the sound, Nicholas could feel the reverberation of Alex's sneezes. The fabric and cotton did little to stop the noise, too, so he pulled his pillow off his face and looked at Alex, watching him sneeze again. "You all right?"

Alex nodded. His arm was outstretched, and his nose scrunched in anticipation of more. Obviously, his ability to speak was limited. He'd woken with the sneezing fit and it had continued for another five minutes after. Mornings like this weren't even unusual. For an entire week, Alex had been tortured with allergies. When he woke up, when he fell asleep, when he was trying to pack their lunches for the day...endlessly. As a result, Nicholas had to put up with the sneezes also.

He'd tried to tune the sound out, but Alex was a notoriously loud sneezer. At one point, he joked they'd get a noise complaint from the neighbors if Alex didn't manage to get over this. Still, the sneeze he'd known was coming shook his body. "All right, I'm up," Nicholas said, kissing Alex's shoulder. There was no chance he'd be going back to sleep at this point. As he stood, he grazed his fingers along the side of Alex's face. "I'm going to go make you some tea." He adjusted his pillow back into place, silently cursing the fabric for not drowning out the noise better. Instead of sleeping, he could at least try to make Alex feel better. "Wait here."

Alex nodded in response again, sneezing right after. The redness around his nose was a clear indicator he was miserable, which Alex confirmed with "my nose burns." Soft tissues could only get someone so far when they were constantly wiping their nose.

"I know. I'll get the moisturizer after the tea," Nicholas promised, heading for the kitchen. The sneezes continued as Nicholas waited for the kettle to whistle. Shaking his head, he mumbled to himself, "It's going to be a long spring." He dropped a sugar cube into the bottom of a mug and flinched as he heard another sneeze from the bedroom. "Bless you," he called. Herbal tea was the right solution, one meant for fighting sickness, and he filled the infuser carefully before dropping it into the mug beside the sugar. Alex's continued sneezing was so loud Nicholas was surprised it wasn't rattling the dishes in the kitchen. Every once in a while, Alex would stop for a few minutes, long enough to catch his breath, but would inevitably start up again, not to mention he had an awful cough that wouldn't help matters at all. As Nicholas discarded the tea leaves into the trash, he wondered how much longer Alex would be this miserable.

"Here," he said, entering the bedroom, mug in hand. "Drink up."

Alex took the mug, looking at the contents. "Thank you." His voice was strained from the drainage, throat raw from his cough.

"How do you feel?" Nicholas asked him.

"Great." The sarcasm in Alex's voice was palpable, the exhaustion evident. "I think I've got a summer cold." The words were almost hard to make out given his congestion, the little slur in his voice, and the soft struggle to pronounce certain letters without the use of his nose.

"First of all," Nicholas said, rubbing his back gently, "it's not summer yet. Second, I think you're still not used to all the pollen in Omaha." Nicholas remembered all too well how stuffed up he'd been when they visited Alex's mom in LA and he was breathing different air than he was used to. There, his own sinuses felt like they were full of gelatin or some other nasty, viscous stuff. "Give it time. You won't be this miserable next spring, I'm sure."

"It's been more than a year! I've been here so long! I'm used to the freakin' air," Alex protested, but he sneezed again, sloshing tea onto his foot. "Ugh."

"Clearly, the pollen hates you. Or you hate it. I'm not really sure which one."

"It's a mutual thing," Alex said, staving off another attack long enough to take a sip of the tea Nicholas had bought. "Gosh. I'm so gross."

"Bless you," Nicholas told him, even though he hadn't sneezed this time. One was coming. He knew that much. "You're never gross, sweetheart. Drink your tea." He reached across him and handed Alex another tissue from the bedside table, a clean one from the box that was surrounded by a smattering of used tissues. He made a mental note to bring a trash can in, to place by the bedside.

Alex's eyes were red-rimmed and glassy, and he looked dazed and over-exhausted. For good reason too. They were both drained from the entire situation. Aside from staying home in bed, Nicholas wasn't sure Alex should be up doing anything. He'd already mentioned lightheadedness, and he needed the rest. But Nicholas knew if he suggested that, he'd be met with an eyeroll and an "I'm fine." He kept his mouth shut. Alex would figure it out himself at some point or another, or he'd wear himself out and take a nap.

A quick glance at the bedside clock earlier had shown him Alex's allergies had woken them before six. Now? It was barely seven. Nicholas couldn't stifle his yawn. "Are you good in here?" he asked Alex. If nothing else, he could focus on preparing lunch for later or cleaning the apartment. He didn't have better plans this early on a Saturday morning.

Alex sneezed and this time the tea spilled on his leg. Nicholas was happy the herbal tea didn't require a high water temperature. Alex nodded. "I'm fine."

I know him too well. Of course, Alex would say he was fine.

"Clearly you're not. Not fine enough. Let me take the tea until you can drink it." Nicholas took the mug from his hand and set it on the bedside table.

"Thank you," Alex said, but with his stuffy nose, the words came out more like *thake you* instead. "I guess you can give me my tea back sometime next century then. I'm never going to stop sneezing."

"How about a shower? Would that help?"

"Are you coming on to me?" Alex grinned, raising an eyebrow and bumping Nicholas with his shoulder.

"Absolutely, if you're expecting a hot date with some eucalyptus and spearmint. But if you meant you wanted me to be in there, sure. I'll join. Just, uh, no...no funny business," he said, laughing. "I'm trying to make you feel better, but not *that* much better. Not until you get better overall."

Alex nodded in agreement. "Okay. Eucalyptus, spearmint, and you. That sounds like a great plan. Even if you are absolutely no fun at all right now." He leaned in and kissed Nicholas's cheek. "Better if I don't get you sick."

Nicholas snorted and then turned and grabbed Alex's jaw, guiding his chin until they were facing each other. He kissed him properly and pulled away so Alex could breathe again. His nose wasn't conducive to proper airflow right now, which kept their kisses short and sweet. "You aren't contagious, sweetheart. Allergies."

"It's a cold!" Alex protested. "I *am* contagious." The argument was never-ending.

"Are colds contagious anyway?" Nicholas mused. Alex was already standing and shedding a trail of clothes as he made a beeline for the bathroom, and Nicholas swatted him on the rear gently as he passed. "They're about as contagious as allergies are, dork," he muttered, smirking. Either way, cold or allergies, they were at least going to get in a nice hot shower. That was the part Nicholas was looking forward to.

*

Alex had to admit the eucalyptus and spearmint disk Nicholas placed in the bottom of the shower helped. For one, Nicholas was in the shower with him. That always helped. It had nothing to do with the disk though. Even if he didn't feel up to doing anything more than simply appreciating the impossibly tall, lean man in front of him, he was thankful for his fiancé's presence in the shower. He was handsome, but also the congestion's effect on his ability to breathe turned into lightheadedness. Having Nicholas's hands to keep him upright kept him safer in the slippery, confined space. He also appreciated Nicholas's help bending down to place the disk on the floor so he didn't have to. Every time he bent forward himself, he got dizzy, and snot threatened to spill out of his nose and drip onto the tile. The idea of that grossed him out. Sure, letting his snot flow freely in the shower was better than letting it go anywhere else, but not bending at all, not dripping, was even better.

"See? It's amazing how much free space we have with a clean shower," Alex said, laughing as Nicholas put the scented disk down near their feet, a few inches away from the holes of the drain.

"Alex, my darling. Love of my entire life. You cleaned the shower out two days after you moved in. Do you not think that *maybe* bringing this up almost a year later is a little bit excessive?" Nicholas grinned and raised an eyebrow, and Alex cracked up, laughing so hard he clutched his chest.

"Oh, the way you don't still mock me for my favorite Christmas movies?" Alex asked. "I think you don't appreciate my hard work enough," he snarked, but that was a joke too. So many things between them were, for the most part, just jokes. They'd had their serious squabbles, but this wasn't one of them. Nicholas *was* appreciative, in a million different ways. He'd told Alex he loved the clean shower and how the organization made him happy, and how the shelves made finding his favorite products easier, having only his favorite seasonally scented wash in the shower with the rest underneath the sink behind the bath towels.

But Nicholas had rarely stopped at merely telling Alex he appreciated him. He often showed him, too, again and again in the shower. Thinking about the things they could be doing had Alex wishing he felt well enough for that again: Nicholas's kisses down his neck, and hands sliding down his back, fingers twining, and hands tangled in hair, soft gasps barely audible over the water running down them. He pushed the thought away so he wouldn't get needy during this shower.

"Don't I appreciate you?" Nicholas asked, grinning like a fool, as if reading Alex's mind. Not that it would be hard. His blood was rushing to the part of his body that made it clear what he'd been thinking about. "Turn around then. I'll appreciate you thoroughly," Nicholas said, voice a low growl. This was the fun of teasing him about the shower. Alex liked what happened when he gave Nicholas trouble, and the way they would handle that trouble.

Alex considered asking again if Nicholas was coming onto him, but he didn't. Instead, he turned obediently, waiting as Nicholas grabbed eucalyptus shampoo from the shelf Alex had picked out for the shower several months before. The installation was neat and apartment-friendly, keeping the bottles organized and off the floor. As Nicholas massaged the shampoo into his hair, working it into a lather, Alex perked up. "I can smell it."

"I would hope so," Nicholas laughed. "It's pretty strong stuff."

"No. Nicholas. Listen to me. I can *smell* it. That means it's working!" For the first time in days, Alex could properly smell out of both of his nostrils. He took deep breaths, appreciating the oxygen intake through his nose, giving his chapped, dry lips a break from trying to breathe through them instead. Relief didn't begin to cover how he felt. The ability to detect the minty aroma, for steam to penetrate the throbbing congestion in his head? Divine. His sense of smell was a gift from another world.

"Good. Relax, then. Breathe."

Alex loved the way Nicholas's hands moved against his scalp, sudsing the shampoo into his hair, relaxing him completely. His fingertips worked their way down, gentle and soft, washing the abdominal muscles Alex had been overusing every time he sneezed. "Better?" Nicholas finally asked.

"Better." He hadn't sneezed during the entire shower, and thankfully, the shower tablet was fully dissolved. He turned around and kissed Nicholas's cheek again. He'd rather play it safe when it came to germs.

Even as he got dressed, he continued to smile. Breathing felt nice. Not breathing the soupy thick air of the shower was even better. Now, he could smell the cold herbal tea Nicholas had made him, and the strong unlit candle on the bedside table, one Nicholas had ordered from a small farm shop in Texas in Alex's favorite scent.

As he leaned down to put his socks on—new, bright springtime socks Nicholas got for him as a joke—a rush of discomfort hit him. The gunk all shifted back into place, filling his sinuses again. He looked up at Nicholas, his eyes watering.

And then he sneezed.

"Crap."

Chapter Two

Vivid Plans

"You can't live in the shower," Nicholas said, laughing.

"I can. I *will*." Alex stamped his foot playfully, rolling his eyes. The shower was the only place he'd felt better since his entire fit of congestion hit him as spring arrived.

"Go on, then," Nicholas said, swatting him on the butt with a dishtowel. "Go breathe or whatever." He smirked. The constant showering made him grateful water was included in their rent. Never mind that they weren't saving the planet during this stretch of him being ill. So long as Alex could breathe, that was what mattered most to him.

He watched as Alex headed for the bedroom, sneezing again. Every sneeze now made him think of the stand-up comics they'd see on Friday nights, any show they could get cheap tickets to at the last minute, and all the jokes they'd made about husbands faking sickness for sympathy and alone time. All of it made him wonder whether the heterosexuals were even okay? Did they even *like* their spouses? Because Alex was definitely, truly, very sick. He wished he could fix it, to make him better, and he knew Alex wanted to feel better too. Allergy medicine hadn't helped, and Nicholas wondered if Alex was right. Maybe this really *was* a spring cold.

The only real solution he knew for a cold was homemade soup, his mother's chicken and dumplings, Southern-style comfort in a bowl. His mother's recipe was special; instead of dumplings made with water, these were made with broth. Bits of onion, shredded chicken, and herbs—relics of the broth, captured like fossils—flecked into the dough, making it richer and tastier than any he'd had in a restaurant. Who cared that it wasn't ten in the morning yet? When his fiancé was sick, time didn't matter. Making chicken and dumplings to cure his aching sinuses mattered, even if they ate it as a late breakfast instead of the traditional dinner.

When he was growing up, Nicholas's mom had instilled in him that chicken and dumplings were the cure to darn near any ailment. It made sense. Every time she would make it for his childhood colds or his dad's nasty flu, they would recover like magic. It made less sense for when she'd make the meal for random ailments, like the time he fell off his scooter and skinned both knees and his hands, but he imagined that was more about having an excuse to make chicken and dumplings than anything else. Either way, Nicholas considered the dish to be the ultimate comfort food.

He brought the water to a boil, chicken bobbing around the water as he seasoned it carefully. Onions, butter, herbs: everything he added made the broth taste better. He added fresh garlic, certain it was the answer to making Alex's allergies disappear, even if it hadn't worked for him yet. He was sure this, along with the vegetable scraps from the freezer he used for flavor, would make a broth that would go head-to-head with Alex's sneezing. At least he hoped so. If his mother was right, this could cure any ailment.

All Alex had to do was take Nicholas's advice to rest and eat up.

As he stirred the broth and drained the vegetable scraps, he listened for more sneezes, but he didn't hear any. Instead, he heard the shower turn on yet again. "Good," he muttered, even though Alex had just gotten out. "That'll help." The steam opened his nasal passages, calming his sneezes down, but only for the duration of the shower. Nicholas had to wonder what would happen when Alex had to go back to work on Monday morning, and back to class. He couldn't exactly bring the shower with him so, short of a full box of Kleenex, Nicholas was certain he'd be miserable.

Waiting for the broth to start boiling again, Nicholas opened his wedding binder. He leaned against the counter and flipped through the pages. As he turned the pages, some of the glossy magazine images began to turn up at the edges. He reached for a glue stick and stuck down one of the pictures, an emerald velvet tux that looked like it would match Alex's eyes beautifully.

Nicholas knew he'd gotten lucky. So far, Alex had been on board with every lavish plan, though he'd joked more than once about eloping. Nicholas knew some of Alex's protests weren't a joke, that Alex did want to forego the drama of an extensive event, but he always came around to Nicholas's plans anyway. Nicholas was appreciative of that.

He'd spent his entire life dreaming about the perfect wedding—or most of it. When other teens were focused on the ACTs, he was getting bridal magazines...and cutting the brides out of the pictures. Not that he didn't have a good ACT score. He did. He'd gotten into the best software engineering program in a three-state radius. But his mind was focused on other aspects of his future the whole time. Who he'd meet. Who he'd marry. Who he'd spend his life with. His parents had never fallen out of love, madly focused on each other until the day his father died, and his mom hadn't remarried.

To him, eternal love was real. Eternal love was more important than anything else, to be treasured and found and captured somehow. A love like that endured through death and even beyond it, he believed. As he skimmed through the binder, looking at the pictures, he thought of Alex, and the love they shared, and he had no doubt they belonged together. "It's going to be perfect."

Nicholas looked at the details, at all the plans they should be figuring out this month, twelve months ahead of their wedding date. They'd set the date they wanted in January. That was the main item to check off the list. But now, he was trying to decide between three engagement photographers, and it had been brutal. He flipped to a page and looked back and forth between sample photographs, labeled with keywords to describe their style, their price range, and their location. No matter how long he studied them, he couldn't decide. There were too many good features of each one he'd been considering. He'd picked them for a reason, narrowed down from a much longer list.

"Oh! Shoot!" Broth bubbled over the sides of the pan, spilling onto the stove, startling Nicholas with a sharp hiss and sizzle once it reached the burner. He slid his book aside and turned off the burner, blotting at the mess with a towel and trying not to burn his fingers in the process. Some of the broth fried to the burner, blackening and sticking in a sloppy, crisp mess. "Dang it!" He'd been in his own little world.

"Is something burning?" Alex asked, sniffing the air. Towel-drying his hair, he walked closer into the kitchen and cocked his head to one side.

"Look who can breathe!" Nicholas said, smiling and turning to look at him before glancing back at the mess he'd made of the stove. "Nothing's burning. Well, something *is* burning. Some broth spilled over, but it's all right." He swiped at it again, scratching at part of the burnt, blackened mess and jerking his finger away the second his brain registered the stovetop was still hot. "How are you? Any relief yet?" He tossed the rag aside, giving up on cleaning up until the surface cooled. He could finish the meal on another burner, he supposed.

"The shower helped," Alex said. He sniffed again. The tell-tale stuffiness was already starting to return. "But nothing's burning," he added. "That's a good thing."

"Nothing's burning," Nicholas confirmed.

"Nothing except my love for you. Burning in a good way." Alex winked awkwardly, both eyes closing before he could get it quite right. Still, it was an attempt, and Nicholas cracked up.

"Oh, yeah? You my hunka hunka burning love, there, baby?"

"Only always," Alex asked. "Thank you, thank you very much." Even his best Elvis impression wasn't very good, but Nicholas adored his effort, kissing his nose gently. "You making chicken and dumplings?"

"Guilty as charged," Nicholas said. He pulled Alex closer, wrapping his arms around him and giving him a proper kiss, one hand on his hip as he flicked his tongue over Alex's lower lip and then nuzzled his nose gently.

"I was trying not to get you sick," Alex said, mumbling as he pulled back.

"Baby. It's allergies. You can't get me sick." Nicholas kissed him again. "Don't worry about it."

"If I'm not sick, why are you making chicken and dumplings?" Alex asked, head cocked to one side.

"Because it's going to make you feel better regardless. And it tastes good." Nicholas stuck his tongue out at Alex. "And if I do get sick? Whatever. Sounds worth it to me." He savored another kiss in the rare moment before Alex would be too stuffed up to breathe, the narrow window where they wouldn't have to cut kisses short for him to inhale through his mouth.

"You're cocky," Alex mumbled against his lips, sliding his arms up Nicholas's back to his shoulders before he pulled away and sneezed again. "Dang it!"

Nicholas sighed and pulled away, smiling. "Well, it was worth a try." He focused on his broth again, moving it to the clean burner and turning the heat to low. He'd clean the other half later. "Are you up to looking at something really quick?"

"Yeah, sweetheart, of course." He rested his hand on Nicholas's back. "What's up? Need my opinion on your broth seasoning?"

"No." Nicholas shook his head. "I'm still torn on the engagement photography." He passed the binder across the space between them. "I love this one—Smith and Jones—and how they're using flowers and magic-inspired elements. They'd create a themed shoot that would be brilliant and whimsical."

"That's beautiful," Alex agreed. "What kind of theme are you thinking you'd want? Or would you tell them to go nuts?"

"I was thinking we could do a fun *Singin' in the Rain* kind of thing. Kissing under an umbrella, rain falling down over it, bright rain boots?" He smiled thinking of it, eyes closed to picture how they'd look. "They've done some really cool water effects, and their website makes it look like they have ideas to do that kind of shoot on sunnier days, too, so we could make an appointment and not worry about waiting for rain."

"I love that idea."

Nicholas loved that Alex was always sincere when it came to planning, kind and excited even though he preferred something smaller than Nicholas was interested in. He appreciated the fact that Alex was getting into the wedding plans regardless. Still, decisions weren't as easy as telling him the idea for the first photographer. "There's this other photographer though," he said, stopping him before Alex could pick the first one without seeing the other choices. He wanted to give all the ideas a fair shot.

"Okay. What's the other one?"

"Vivid Portraiture. They do milk baths really well, and they're very on-trend right now and—"

"Milk baths?" Alex asked, peering at the images pasted in the notebook, one of which was a bearded man who looked quite a bit like Nicholas—but not as handsome, Alex would tell him—in a milky-white bath, swirled with blue and purple dyes, strategically placed flowers floating over him. He crinkled his nose.

"Yeah. With the milk, and the floating flowers, and—"

"Baby, I'm stopping you right there. I don't think our family or friends are going to want pictures of us naked in a bath, regardless of us being hidden under milk." He giggled. "I'd prefer my mother not seeing you naked and covered in flowers."

"All right, we'll rule Vivid out then." Nicholas didn't mind crossing them off the list. He loved them, but Alex was right. Wrong shoot for the wrong time. He tried not to let it get to him.

"Not out," Alex said. "Save that one for later. I may not want my mother to see it, but I think you naked and covered in flowers is right up my alley. We could see what their prices are and do this for each other. They've got my vote, just not for our engagement announcements." He smiled sincerely, grazing Nicholas's cheek with his thumb. "And don't you dare think about getting rid of their information. I'm serious. I really do want a shoot like that. Put it in the post-wedded-bliss tab."

"Okay. Thank you, Alex," Nicholas answered. "That narrows us down to two photographers then. Majestic Images does a lot of smoke-themed photo shoots." He turned back to the binder and flipped the page. "See?" Images dotted the page, rainbow-colored smoke in front of same-sex couples.

"Well, at least I don't have to ask if this one is okay with gay couples. Is the first one aware of the fact that we're two men marrying each other? Because if not, the problem of deciding might sort itself out."

The reality was, even as the country grew leaps and bounds, and while their entire friend group was primarily queer, not all of Omaha was as accepting as the people in their little bubble. In this case, though, he'd already checked them out. "I found both of them at the LGBT Wedding Expo last month."

"Good. Then I vote that we go with your *Singin' in the Rain* concept, and you pick whatever photographer is going to execute that better." He rubbed Nicholas's back and looked back and forth. "If you really love the smoke idea, hire them for our wedding and we can do some brilliant wedding pictures like that, or use them for custom thank-you cards or whatever."

Nicholas beamed. Alex was trying very hard to make sure Nicholas got everything he wanted. "Okay. Decision made then. Smith and Jones for the save-the-date and engagement announcements, Majestic for the thank-you cards, and Vivid for our own private purposes."

"Is it really narrowing it down if our narrowing was all three, but for different purposes?" Alex teased as he grabbed a spoon and tasted the broth. Nicholas tried to stop him, to warn him he hadn't salted the meal yet, but he still caught the look on Alex's face that said something wasn't right with the flavor.

"Of course, it is. I had about twenty photographers in my initial list. Picking three? We've done good," Nicholas said.

"We have." Alex gave Nicholas's shoulder a small squeeze. "I'm going to go work on my research and leave you to the broth."

"Good. I'll bring you a bowl in a little bit."

Nicholas swiped at the still-too-hot substance coating the stove with a wet rag, smiling to himself and humming the "Wedding March." Yeah, he had the best fiancé in the world.

Chapter Three

The Great Debate

An hour after they'd made their decision, Alex returned to the kitchen to see the wedding book opened on the counter to the same page they'd been on before, with Nicholas rolling the dumplings out and dropping them into the boiling broth as he stole glances at the page. "Haven't decided yet?" he asked.

"I'm scared I'm going to regret what I go with because the other one would have been better for a specific aspect of the wedding. I've got this—I don't know—crippling fear that I'll think I picked the perfect one for the engagement photos and find out later the other one is better at engagements and this one is better for weddings, or vice versa." He looked away, sighing.

"Nicholas. Instead of telling you we should elope, because then *none* of this would matter in the slightest, because I know you won't go for that option, I'm going to tell you this: whoever you pick is going to do a brilliant job. We'll never get it figured out if you panic about every decision. This is the second choice of the whole wedding. The date? That was easy. But this part?" He kissed

Nicholas's shoulder. "In the long run, we get beautiful pictures either way. Look at these samples. We're going to love them. Call and book them before you change your mind, or I'll call and book them. Okay?"

"Okay," Nicholas said, chewing his lip.

Alex could sense the uneasiness in Nicholas's tone, the way he was agreeing but not really agreeing to what Alex had said. "Not okay. Talk to me."

"What if I love the one who does our save-the-date photos so much that I end up resenting the person doing our wedding photos and thank-you photos?" he asked, biting his lip as he studied the sample pictures again.

"Then you book the save-the-date photographer for our wedding and we get the other photographer to do baby photos instead," Alex said simply. *Eloping would be so much less trouble*. He stuffed the thought away. Eloping wasn't an option, not for Nicholas. Not for someone who had dreamed of a fancy wedding his entire life.

Nicholas frowned and flipped between the pages, keeping his finger in the page to mark it as he went back and forth again.

"Nicholas, I promise you we don't have to stress about this," Alex reminded him. "Anyone you choose will do an amazing job. You've narrowed an impossible list down to the best of the best, so from there? It's all incredible. No one is going to mess up your careful planning and no one is going to ruin our wedding. It's going to be all right." Alex kissed his shoulder and gave him a squeezing hug. "It's going to be just fine," he repeated.

Nicholas nodded. "You're right. It'll be okay. I'm going to email the save-the-date photographer today before I can change my own mind."

Alex pulled out his phone, opened an email, and waved it in front of Nicholas's face. "How about you do it now? You'll keep second-guessing until you do."

Nicholas smiled, took the phone, and sent an email. He could have done so with his own phone, but using Alex's meant that if he changed his mind, he'd have to admit that to Alex personally to email them back. "I wish you didn't know me so well."

"I know you well enough to not want to lose you to an early heart attack, which is exactly what's going to happen if you work yourself into a tizzy over every single step of this process. This is the first real decision we have to make and you're already tense." Alex rubbed at the tension in his back, working his hands on Nicholas's shoulders.

"I don't want to settle for okay." Nicholas shrugged into the massage and furrowed his brow. "I didn't settle for okay on the groom, and I don't want to settle for it on anything else."

"You're not settling. But if you keep thinking you are, you're going to be miserable on our wedding day, and that's the last thing I want. I want for our wedding to be a happy day," Alex said. The twinges of stuffiness were returning to his voice, his ever-present congestion in full form now that he was this far removed from his last shower.

"I'm not miserable. I'm not stressed out," he promised, closing the binder and turning his focus back to the dumplings he was making.

"You seem stressed out." Alex wrapped his arms around Nicholas and nuzzled against his back. Nicholas *was* stressing, and Alex could read it all over his face.

Nicholas rested one floury hand on top of Alex's hands. "I just want our wedding to be perfect."

"I do too. I'm marrying the best man I've ever known, which is why I'm assuming it will be as perfect as I imagine it," Alex said, smiling.

"For a moment, I thought you were leaving it at 'I'm marrying the best man,' and I'd have to call things off!" Nicholas started to laugh, and it turned to a full-fledged cackle as a result.

"Brat," Alex answered, leaving Nicholas to his dumplings as he turned away to go study.

*

Tugging the blankets over his head, Alex groaned. He hated admitting he was too sick to go to work. Calling in? That seemed like a waste of a day. Class, he could get notes for, but work was simply a missed shift, and that wasn't fair to his coworkers either. No way. He couldn't skip. Even when Nicholas brought him his tea, he tried sitting up and getting out of bed, but Nicholas gently pushed him back against the headboard again.

"Let me call in for you," Nicholas said.

"I'm fine." Alex's congestion made it clear he wasn't. The sneezing had stopped, for the most part, but his face was swollen from the congestion in his sinuses and he couldn't breathe out of either side. "I can make it."

"Yeah, and then you can drip snot in everyone's coffee. Great plan. Let's get the entire neighborhood sick."

Nicholas rubbed his leg and teased his fingers through his hair.

"So, what am I going to do instead?" Alex hated feeling lazy more than anything. There was nothing worse than lying in bed, unproductive. During his worst bouts of depression, he still felt the need to do *something*. Usually, that snapped him out of his mood, convincing himself he'd accomplished an important task. Now, though, he wasn't depressed, and he had ideas of what he needed to do: go to work, wash the dishes, work on the next part of his thesis, and make sure the last of the Christmas decorations were completely gone, since it was March. Nicholas had been reluctant to put them away, and he'd only recently convinced him they could decorate for Easter if they'd put the rest of the decorations in the top of the closet where they belonged. He had things he *needed* to do, and as of the night before, he'd been stuck in bed, too miserable to do them.

"Give yourself one day to rest and tackle the world tomorrow," Nicholas answered. "I don't know, Alex. What did you do when you were home sick from school?"

"I didn't get sick like this as a kid." Alex shrugged. "I had perfect attendance."

"Well, then. What did you do during undergrad when you were hungover?"

"Went to class with a headache."

Nicholas snorted. "Everyone thinks I'm an overachiever because I bake a lot and get into the holidays but look at you. Do you ever take a break?" He knew the answer to that already.

"No," Alex said. He equated doing nothing to being worth nothing, the constant pressure to translate productivity into success. Even during his gap year, taking time off to care for his mother, he kept himself fully occupied. He cleaned the house top to bottom twice and talked to his mother and continued researching the topics he loved most. If he wasn't productive, anxiety crept in, tugging at the tendrils of his mind; he knew the habit was horrible. *Not good enough. Do-nothing Alex. Waste of space.* Alex couldn't afford the negative self-talk. He'd dealt with enough frustration about how unproductive he'd been lately, but he was out of patience with himself, done giving himself grace. Slacking wasn't in his vocabulary. Not that he was slacking; he was doing necessary healing.

"I'm going to tell you what most people do. They park their butt on the couch, watch *The Price is Right*, and drink tea and chicken broth."

Alex looked away. "I can't do that." He knew he needed to. His body needed to heal. But his brain wouldn't line up with that. "I'll stay home from work," he finally said. The last thing he wanted was to be responsible for anyone else getting sick. "I'm still going to study though." He wasn't letting school slip. Not when he needed a job. His future husband had a giant inheritance and a strong drive to perform. That was great, up until the point Nicholas seemed to think that was a reason Alex didn't *have* to push, like he could support him. For a lot of guys, maybe having someone to look after them financially would be great. But he wanted an equal, not a sugar daddy. Not that Nicholas ever claimed the role, but the hints had been there, that he could afford not to try as hard because Nicholas had a safety net. What happened if that disappeared though? And where was the personal satisfaction in relying on someone else's money? "Yeah.

Actually, the more I think about it, the better that works out. I have to finish this project."

"Studying is a fair compromise. As long as there's no snotty coffee being served," Nicholas said, smiling. "Drink your tea." He leaned forward and kissed his cheek. "I'm going to work. I'll be back."

Alex nodded. "Love you," he mumbled. "I'll...be here, I guess."

As soon as the apartment was empty, the intrusive thoughts kicked in, and he stood up, holding on to the bed to manage his dizziness, and moved slowly toward the shower.

Chapter Four

Information Overload

Alex tried to do whatever he could to avoid the thoughts plaguing him as he stared at the ceiling in his room. He'd gone back to bed instead of getting dressed after this shower, and now he felt guilty.

You're not working hard enough.

You should be productive.

Why aren't you doing anything?

Hard work makes your body stronger.

If you're really sick, the cure for it is harder work.

All of those were phrases his grandfather would say during long hot summers at his house. "Get off your ass," Alex muttered to himself, "you're burning daylight." He pried himself out of the bed and tugged on shorts, then headed for the kitchen. He felt like a good-for-nothing waste of space, sick and therefore completely not worth energy or effort.

His head was too full and congested for him to get his thesis written. Every word trudged through the wreckage and sludge in his brain to get to the page, and when he read back over them, none of the words were good enough. So, he stood and he wandered, he checked emails, and he headed back to the kitchen. The dishes were done. "Thanks, Nicholas," he snarked.

Nicholas had only tried to help. Alex knew that. But a tiny part of him felt annoyance with him for taking away a task Alex could have done. "Petty," he reminded himself. He grazed the countertops, finding Nicholas's wedding binder. *Their* wedding binder. Even though Nicholas had been carefully working on it since he was a teen, it represented their wedding ceremony. He had every right to look, and Nicholas had never stopped him. Heck, Nicholas passed it to him to look at from time to time.

He opened the pages, finding pictures of tuxedo inspiration, little notes next to images like "matches Alex's eyes," or "this would look pretty with the peonies." Each page was so clearly *Nicholas*. The downside was that meant the wedding was very much not Alex. The entire plan looked overwhelming and high-effort—not in the way that made Alex feel productive, but the kind of way that induced anxiety, like they'd be taking pictures for hours before the ceremony and he wondered if they'd be able to enjoy the parts that mattered. "Of course, you will," Alex reminded himself. "You're marrying the love of your life, and it's going to be perfect."

He flipped to the next page, with *Twelve Months Before* carefully written out. That was where they were now, one year before their wedding.

Set the Date. A tiny checkmark next to it and their date handwritten beside that showed they'd completed the task.

Set your Budget. Nicholas had helpfully written "Money is no object," next to that one, but then he had written a price range beside that. *$35,000*. Alex flinched at the number. Nicholas's inheritance was large, and this would barely make a dent in it, but Alex had grown up much leaner. The rent costs in LA ate up most of his family's monthly income, and after his mother and stepfather divorced, they'd struggled more, even as his mother picked up multiple jobs. When she'd lost one of them due to her depression and refusal to leave her bed, Alex had picked up the slack. The idea of blowing what he'd make in a year on one single event blew his mind. "Breathe. It isn't like there isn't money for it," he reminded himself. The idea took some getting used to.

Choose your Theme. They'd been back and forth on that for a while, as evidenced by the tabbed dividers on the side with different themes, and entire wedding drafts for each. Farmhouse, which Alex wasn't keen on because it reminded him of his grandfather's farm and the frustration which went with it. Rustic, which went hand in hand with Farmhouse but wasn't quite so hard for him to stomach. Gay, which simply leaned into the queer theme, and was Alex's preference. After being quiet about who he was for far too long, "gay" conveyed the Big Fat Homosexual Wedding of His Dreams, or so he'd described it that way to Nicholas. Nicholas, however, was currently leaning toward Rustic. Tropical had been nixed from the get-go. Nicholas was too worried a random hurricane would delay their plans; Alex reminded him that tornadoes and flooding posed a real threat in Omaha, but it hadn't swayed him away from wanting a local wedding. So no, they hadn't chosen a theme yet. Nicholas fretted about that fact on a nightly basis. There was also the option for Pastel, but Pastel was less of a theme and more of a color scheme, in Alex's mind.

Organize Engagement Party

Find a Florist

Research Catering Options

Decide on Officiant

The list went on for an entire page, overwhelming him with the number of tasks they needed to get done before the month was over. If Alex weren't feeling sick already, he'd be sick now; they had so much to do in such a short amount of time.

How would they find the time for these things? Sure, some tasks wouldn't take that long, like deciding on an officiant, but he had school, a thesis to finish, papers to write...not to mention his job. And Nicholas didn't have it much easier. After graduating early, he'd taken on a teaching fellowship at the school, moving up from his TA job. He was busy. When he wasn't planning their wedding, he was grading papers, and the idea of throwing more at their already strapped lives was too much. By this time next year, Nicholas would probably be well on his way to finishing his five-year plan, because he was just that kind of guy. And Alex? Hopefully, he'd be graduating, finding a new job that was actually in his field. But to add in all these details, and the months and months of planning? Every note and checklist item made Alex's head spin. How would they work it all in?

In theory, Alex wanted Nicholas to have the wedding of his dreams, even if that didn't line up with Alex's idea of a good wedding day. But in practice, the whole thing exhausted him. He could tell squeezing everything in to make the celebration Nicholas's idea of perfect was a migraine waiting to happen on what should be a happy day. He wasn't quite sure how to make sure Nicholas got what he needed, without losing his mind trying to give him that.

Jerking to attention when the door swung open and he heard the telltale thud of Nicholas's bag on the floor nearby, Alex snapped the book closed, backing up in his chair as if he'd been caught with his hand in the cookie jar, or watching porn or something. He knew that was silly, but the sense of guilt remained.

"Hey, sweetheart," Nicholas said, kissing his head. "Looking through all our plans?"

Alex relaxed. "I was just, uh, seeing if there was anything I could help with while you were at work." He looked up at Nicholas, reached for his hand, and gave it a squeeze. "Hey, um. Quick question for you. Why the *heck* do we need to pick our rings now? Isn't that early?"

"We don't have to buy them yet," Nicholas explained patiently. "We just need to pick them out so the jeweler has plenty of time to size them, or if we wanted some kind of custom engraving, then there's time for all of that to happen."

Alex nodded, listening intently. "Okay, so if we get them and they're resized, and then in a month I've gained ten pounds from your cooking, I have to get my ring resized all over again?"

"Then we have more time to resize it," Nicholas said, kicking his shoes off and rubbing at one of his feet.

"So...why not buy it later, then get it sized when we do?" Alex threw his head back in frustration. "I know we have to accomplish some of this stuff a certain amount of time in advance, but this is overwhelming." He leaned back in his chair, balancing it on two legs and looking at Nicholas, studying his face. "Even checking off what we've already figured out—the wedding date, the budget, all of that—it feels like we're drowning, especially when we throw in like...stuff that's not about the wedding. I still have a job and school; you have a job and a job search. How does all of that fit in?"

"We have time to get those things done, Alex. Don't stress. Take the fact that we have time as a life preserver, since you're drowning." He leaned toward Alex and took his hands as Alex set his chair back down on all four legs. "Sweetheart, the love of my life, please do not worry about this." Nicholas was trying, but Alex still tensed up.

"I'm not worrying!" Alex insisted. He opened the notebook again to the list of tasks they had to do this month, sniffling. Maybe they were residual allergy sniffles, but more likely, he was about to cry. "Okay. I am worrying. What can we do this weekend to shorten this list and calm me down?" He was asking a rhetorical question, but he was asking it aloud in case Nicholas had a plan for what came next. "We can probably decide on what style and color we want to wear to make sure we're color coordinating, and uh, we can settle on that theme."

Nicholas stood up and walked around the table. He rubbed Alex's shoulders. "Alex. You are *sick*. Let yourself heal and worry about it later." He closed the book in front of Alex and kissed the sensitive place behind his ear. "How about we go have an afternoon nap? Take that any way you please."

Chapter Five

Burning Love

For the first time in days, Alex felt good enough for them to take it there, so he wasn't using a nap as an opportunity to sleep. He could breathe, thanks to the VapoRub on his chest, but Nicholas had also gotten him worked up, rubbing it on nice and slow. Either way, he was turned on, pulling on Nicholas's shoulder to steal a kiss. "We should do something while I can breathe," he said, and Nicholas nodded.

"Something like what?"

"Something like this." Alex ran his hand down Nicholas's body slowly, dipping it under the waistband of his slacks and teasing along the fabric underneath.

"Oh yeah?"

"Yeah. Like I said, I can breathe."

Nicholas smirked and kissed along Alex's jaw, nipping at his ear. "So can I," he answered, carefully avoiding the mentholated spread he'd rubbed on Alex's chest as he kissed his way down his side. Alex propped his head up on his arm, gazing down at Nicholas. This was the part he loved. Wedding stress aside, cold aside, heck, the whole world aside, he could just enjoy these moments with Nicholas in the quiet of their bedroom. He cracked up laughing as Nicholas kissed his lowest rib. "Whoa there. Beard tickles."

Nicholas smiled up at him and rubbed his beard gently along the skin. "Like this?" he asked, and Alex flinched and jerked and writhed, wiggling away from the touch.

"Yes!" he yelped, prompting more from Nicholas. "You're killing me! Nicky, baby, oh gosh!" He kept squirming until Nicholas stopped, climbed back up, and kissed him.

"I like how ticklish you are," he said softly.

Alex groaned. "You're the only person allowed to tickle me," he finally permitted, squeezing Nicholas on the side in a gentle retaliation tickle. "Come on...now you owe me for tickling me!"

Nicholas laughed. "I owe you, huh?" He slid a hand along Alex's length gently. "How's that? Is this a good repayment?"

"Oh..." Alex moaned. Good was an understatement. He arched his back and fluttered his lashes as Nicholas worked his length gently, flicking a thumb over the head. "Incredible." He could feel a slight tingle and wondered if his lightheadedness was making this moment different... better. He moaned a little louder, body quivering.

Nicholas knew all his best spots and the touches he liked. He knew the ways Alex liked to be talked to and nibbled at. There was a beautiful intensity in the way they intimately knew each other, in the way they'd known each other time and time again since the first time they'd collided.

As his fingertips worked across the tip again, Alex shuddered and focused on the sensations. "Oh. Oh no...oh...wow, okay, that burns actually," he said, biting his lip.

Nicholas jerked back, letting go. "What's wrong? What hurts?"

"It's on fire!" Alex panicked, fanning at himself.

"Fire?" Nicholas scrambled to the bathroom to get a wet rag. He tossed it to Alex, who proceeded to wipe himself in haste, growling in pain and frustration as he did.

Alex looked around, trying to figure out what had gone wrong, why he burned *there*. Did he have a UTI? There wasn't any other option—he and Nicholas weren't seeing anyone else. "What the heck?" His eyes landed on the blue-and-green jar by the bedside table and he burst out laughing through the pain.

"What?"

"The VapoRub. You didn't wash your hands after putting it on me because we got distracted."

"Oh no," Nicholas said. "Oh no. I'm so sorry." He scanned the bed for anything else that might offer relief, but nothing else was helpful. Tissues, some wadded and used, their blankets, cell phone chargers...none of the items offered any kind of aid for the burning Alex experienced.

"I think the washcloth is helping, but uh. Wow, that hurts." He bit his lip and tried to focus on anything but the pain. "Is it uh...you good with me not reciprocating right now?"

"What? No, of *course* you're not doing that now!" Nicholas shouted. "Alex, I almost burnt your...your dick off with Vicks. The last thing you need to be concerned with is turning me on!"

Alex smiled and kissed Nicholas. "Don't worry, I won't find a way to work IcyHot into our bedroom routine either." Nicholas giggled and Alex couldn't help laughing also. So much for using the opportunity while he could breathe. "How about we get another wet washcloth since this one has stuff on it, and then take a nap?"

"A nap sounds excellent right about now."

*

As Nicholas watched the steady rise and fall of Alex's chest, able to breathe for the moment, he thought about how they should have gone straight for the nap. Not only would they be less traumatized by the VapoRub, but the way Alex zonked out as soon as the pain was dulled showed how much he needed rest. At least the VapoRub was good for one thing, if Alex wasn't thoroughly scared off using it forever after this. Nicholas still felt bad for not thinking to wash his hands, even an hour and a half after Alex had dozed off.

He watched as Alex's eyelids twitched and as he mumbled a few unintelligible words in his sleep. He rolled over, closer to Nicholas, head resting on his chest, and Nicholas rubbed his back, thinking about what Alex had said before.

NICHOLAS: *Do you think me planning a big wedding is wrong?*

NICHOLAS: *Like, do you think it's going to cause more harm than good?*

If anyone would know, Jade would. Jade knew him better than anyone, maybe better than Alex in some ways. And she knew Alex well too. Beyond that, she'd gotten married the fall before. She knew weddings. Well, kind of.

JADE: *Only you know the answer to that.*

JADE: *But there's a reason we ran to Vegas*

JADE: *I couldn't handle all the details*

JADE: *The dresses and the tuxes and the wedding party and the guests and then realizing we wanted you guys to be our wedding party AND our guests and we didn't have other guests planned...*

JADE: *The whole situation was a mess. You know that.*

The texts came in rapid-fire, and Nicholas scrolled through them. He knew the reasons. He knew why she'd been against wedding planning, and he accepted it. Still, he couldn't leave that without a snarky remark; that was just part of the relationship he and Jade had.

NICHOLAS: *Yeah, and I've never forgiven you*

NICHOLAS: *We didn't get to go to your wedding so you're on my do not invite list*

NICHOLAS: *Maybe you can earn your way back if you tell me how to fix my fiancé's cold*

He waited for Jade to text back and he didn't hear anything. Not a question on how Alex was doing, not a message back about his jokes. Nothing.

NICHOLAS: *I'm joking, Jade.*

NICHOLAS: *You both have to be at our wedding.*

He was met with silence on the other end. Jade didn't say anything back. Now he had another concern to stress about. Alex's cold. Alex's unfortunate personal burn. Jade's silent treatment. He bit his lip and considered texting again, but worried that was only taking it too far. Maybe Jade was busy.

A knock at the door jolted him out of his self-pity though. He scrambled to get to it, pulling his clothes back into place and closing the bedroom door behind him so Alex could rest. "Hello?" he asked, swinging the door open.

"Veronica says it's allergies, not a cold," Jade answered, without so much as a hello as she pushed past Nicholas and leaned against the counter.

"Alex insists it *isn't* allergies!" Nicholas laughed. "Okay, so, allergies. We'll try another round of allergy medicine." He shrugged. "What's up?"

"Is he coughing? You can put some VapoRub on his feet for that," she suggested, not answering his question.

"He's not coughing, thankfully. And, uh. I think we're about done with VapoRub for the time being." He tried to compose himself. "Any other ideas?"

"Yeah. Here." Jade reached into her pocket and pulled out a tiny plastic bear. "V says this is a magic cure-all and will fix his stuffy nose in an instant."

"Honey?" Nicholas asked, raising his eyebrow and taking the bottle from her. "Her solution to a sickness that has lasted two weeks is honey?"

"Not just honey," Jade clarified. "*Local* honey. Her friend from work keeps bees as a side gig and he told her the bees get pollen from local trees and flowers and all that. Then they make the honey. When someone eats it, it acts as a sort of immunization against the pollen that gave them nasal crap to begin with." She took a breath, having barely paused during the entire first batch of information, and added, "Here. We're supposed to plant these seeds in pots on our balconies in exchange for the honey sample." She handed him a packet of seeds and a small brochure.

"That sounds counterintuitive," Nicholas said.

"Planting seeds?"

"No. The whole bit about pollen ruining your life so you should willingly spread it on toast. How can that possibly be helpful? If he's allergic to it, won't that make him sicker?" Nicholas flipped the cap open and drizzled a tiny dab on his finger before licking it off. He'd never tasted honey this incredible—sweet and floral with a touch of fruitiness—and he realized that whether it worked or not, he'd probably buy some eventually for the flavor alone.

"I thought the same thing. But he swears by it, and as a result, V swears by it too. Besides, what does it hurt? You really want to throw another box of pills at him? Like you know I'm all for some medication, baby, but if that hasn't helped, why try more of the same?"

Nicholas shook his head. He couldn't disagree with that. If honey had even the smallest chance of working, they would try it. Both of them would get some much-needed sleep in that case, if Alex could stop sneezing. "All right, sure. Thank you. How much do I owe you?"

"Nothing. So long as you plant the seeds."

"Okay. I'll plant the seeds." He hadn't the slightest idea about gardening—they'd already killed two sets of succulents on their balcony that were supposed to be unkillable—but making an attempt to grow them was a small price to pay if the honey worked like she implied it might.

"Oh. Also, you owe me an eternity of friendship, lifelong undying devotion, and overthrowing the reigning governmental overlords."

"Is that all?" Nicholas asked, throwing his head back with a laugh.

"And extra dessert at your wedding, because you'd be a monster to make me choose between chocolate cake or vanilla." Her face was serious, but her voice wasn't.

"I already told you. You're not invited." He pulled his binder out and flipped to the dessert tab. "We haven't scheduled any tastings yet, but I'm not sure what the plan is yet. Maybe we'll do pie instead of cake. Everyone has cake. I thought pie might make our wedding stand out." He hadn't spoken to Alex about it, but he wasn't certain he could stomach cake.

When he'd started making his binder years before, he knew the exact cake he wanted. His aunt had a white almond sour cream cake with a wild berry filling and a vanilla buttercream, and it had blown his mind. He'd come up with every conceivable design to fit every theme, but the flavor had been unchanged. When his mother found out her cancer was certain to stick around, that she'd never beat her long fight with it, he baked white almond sour cream cupcakes for her, filling and frosting them so they could eat them together. *"This will be my wedding cake,"* he'd told her. *"Now you can taste it."* The thought of it made him sad—heck, worse than sad, maybe a giant ball of grief—and he hadn't had white almond sour cream cake since.

"Pie?"

"Yeah. Pie."

Jade flipped through the pages of the binder, past all the cakes he'd carefully pasted in, and then looked up at him. "If you're doing pie, you have to bake it yourself. There isn't a single baker in Omaha who can get a crust flaky enough for your picky ass."

"Shut up!" Nicholas protested, but he knew she was right.

"Second of all, you've got this backed up somewhere, right? You have to have a Pinterest or something going so you don't lose all of this when you inevitably leave it in a coffee shop and it disappears."

"Yes, Jade, I have a lot of ideas saved online," he answered. "The best stuff is in there though. Business cards, phone numbers. You can't back that stuff up on Pinterest, J. Go to a wedding expo and tell me how you plan on putting their brochure on your online vision board."

"I don't know, a scanner maybe?"

"That's not the same. I like to be able to touch it. And the aesthetic! Jade, come on. This is scrapbooked to perfection." Not to mention the parts he and his mother had worked on together. It wasn't simply his wedding binder. The project was an heirloom, a memory of their lives together before she passed away. He couldn't back that up online if he tried. He took the book from her arm and flipped to the front, saying, "Even if I allowed the binder out of my sight—which I don't—I've got my contact information in here so it can be returned. Nice try, small fry. You're *not* going to make me panic about this."

Jade rolled her eyes. "The whole binder plan sounds like a recipe for disaster, Nick."

"Yeah? And you know what about it?" He closed the book, set it aside, and flipped through a wedding magazine. "I'm still salty about not getting to see the loves of my life marry each other."

"I know," Jade conceded, hands in the air in surrender, laughing. "We owe you the full wedding experience."

"Exactly. You do. And anyway, Alex and I are doing it this way so you won't feel left out of our big day," he joked. "But like I said, you aren't invited, brat. V can tell you all about it when she gets home."

"As long as I get some cake, I don't care." She reached forward and hugged him.

"Pie," Nicholas corrected.

"As long as I get *dessert,* I'll be happy," Jade said pointedly. "Here I was, going to go buy out your registry. What ever will I do now?" She exaggerated her Southern accent, snorted, and gave Nicholas a small shrug. "Anyway. I have to go. Try the honey and tell me how much better he is after so I can tell V the news that honey—just as she expected—is the magic cure to allergies."

"And if it doesn't work?"

"Then you'll tell me that the honey—just as expected—is the magic cure," she repeated. "I'm not going to listen to her pull fourteen different obscure studies about why it works. Come on, Nick. Save my marriage and lie to me if you have to."

He laughed and kissed her cheek. "Thanks, Jade. The honey is fantastic. It has cured Alex solely by having a presence in my apartment." Whether or not it worked, the honey tasted good, so he didn't mind regardless.

Chapter Six

The Wedding of Their Dreams

One entire small honey bear, two batches of chicken and dumplings, and ten days later, Alex finally started to feel better. He wasn't great yet, by any means. As much as he appreciated relief, he wasn't back to his normal self, body aching, and nose stuffed. He didn't have the energy to go to the gym either—to stick with the "Hot Husband Routine" he and Nicholas had planned for their workouts—but he could almost breathe, and that was enough.

"The pollen count is down," Nicholas said. "That's why."

"It's not the pollen. I had a cold," Alex argued again. "If it were allergies, the honey would have helped me out six days ago." He rolled his eyes, but he still snorted a laugh.

"Unless Veronica is wrong about how effective the honey is."

"Try telling her that," Alex joked. "See how you fare." He looked up from the papers he had spread across the kitchen table.

"I'm not telling her," he laughed. The printer hummed, background music to their conversation. Every few minutes, the printer whirred again with the sound of more papers passing through. Alex didn't glance up. For months, it hadn't printed out a page of his research or a single sheet of material he needed for his thesis.

No, the printer almost exclusively made that noise for the wedding binder. Alex didn't mind though. He'd already had to move a stack of wedding magazines to sit down. This was his life now, all abuzz about the wedding. He kept telling himself this was the wedding they *both* wanted. Nicholas had painstakingly flipped through the magazines stacked there, lamenting the lack of two-groom weddings on the pages. Either way, there was something comfortable about sitting here and laughing like this, the hum of the machine and Nicholas's quiet, happy mumblings as he glued a boutonniere he'd found to be exceptionally lovely.

"Am I distracting you?" Nicholas asked, looking up from his page.

"Hmm? No." He smiled. "You're good. I'm just trying to get through data encryption algorithms to find some sort of coherent written thought. Trust me, no printer could trip me up. If you were blasting that dang Christmas song, maybe," Alex taunted.

"Will I ever live it down?" Nicholas asked. It had been over a year, but Alex continued to bring up the second time they met, like when he'd turn up the music in the car and say, "Still not as loud as you during the holidays!"

Nicholas laughed. "You could have stayed for pie."

"Yeah, okay, I'll go ahead and venture into the weird stranger's apartment," Alex said. "No way that could bring any horror movie-esque consequences..." He stood up, closed his laptop, and walked over to Nicholas at the desk and wrapped his arms around his shoulders.

"You're marrying the weird stranger, Alex. Should I remind you of that? Again?"

Alex laughed and kissed his neck. "I like the pink one." He pointed to a flower arrangement on the page.

"Mm-hmm, me too." Nicholas turned toward him, and Alex kissed him, one hand on his cheek, his thumb twirling hairs from Nicholas's beard. "I was thinking that putting two or three like this at each table would look really nice and—"

"Nicholas, do we really need so many flowers?" He furrowed his brow and backed up, studying his face seriously. "I... That's a lot of money and energy and time on cut flowers that are dying, and then we'll do what with them after?"

Nicholas's cheeks grew red. "Oh. Okay." He looked back down at his binder, pulling the flowers up off the page, glue still wet. "We'll skip the flowers then."

Alex could see the slump, the way he hunched over the table now, the way he looked away from him. *Ouch*. He'd caused Nicholas pain by being hypercritical again. He took the picture of flowers and smoothed them back down where they'd been before. "Yes, flowers. I didn't say we should skip flowers." Alex pulled back, studying his face and grazing his hand against his cheek. "I meant we could compromise."

Nicholas stood up, leaving his binder open so the glue could dry. He headed for the kitchen, his primary safe space for when he was upset, and Alex knew he'd screwed up. He'd been trying to hold back on the little negative comments, the snips about flowers or expenses or bold weddings. He kept telling himself he could get through one obnoxious day if it meant setting them on the path for the rest of their lives. He'd apologize as soon as Nicholas had space to think in the kitchen. But Nicholas whipped around back to him. "You're not on board with the wedding at all, are you?"

"Nicholas, where is this coming from? What makes you think I'm not okay with our wedding?" He knew where his concern came from, but he thought he'd made it clear he was open to Nicholas's plans regardless.

"You keep going on and on about the expenses and the stress and the decisions I'm making that you hate and...do you even want this to happen?"

Alex had heard a lot about Bridezillas. During his mom's depressive episode, they'd binge-watched a season of a show all about them. He hated to say that his future husband was a little bit of a Groomzilla, but if the polished, black, formal shoe fit... He tensed. "I want the wedding." He could see the tears in Nicholas's eyes. "My criticisms aren't saying I'm not on board with the wedding. I'm merely questioning the sanity of spending this much time on the wedding and this much focus on it, when I get the impression we'll both only be stressed about the outcome." He walked closer to Nicholas and reached for his hand. Nicholas didn't offer his hand in return. A tear fell down his face instead.

"I'm not the one who's stressed! I'm doing most of the planning here, and you're the one who's worried about it."

"Nicholas, babe, you went back and forth on the photos for days. The second we sent the email I could see how concerned you were about whether you made the right choice or not. And then we picked the date, and you moved on to this whole new set of stressors...flowers! Tuxes! Getting the rings *now!*"

"That was *you* who freaked out about everything," Nicholas said.

"Yeah, I stressed about why we had to do them now. You fretted about which one to get because there were too many perfect options, and you had to pick the most perfect one, but what if one of the others was better? I've never seen you second-guess yourself more in your life!" Alex paced, tugging at his hair. This was absolutely ridiculous. Nicholas had to admit he'd been overly stressed about the tasks. Right? Or maybe he didn't have to admit it. Maybe he didn't see that happening. But Alex saw it, and Alex didn't know how to convince him this was a serious issue. "By the time the wedding gets here, I'm worried we won't enjoy it because we'll be too frazzled and sleep-deprived from everything on the checklist! Or that one of us will die of an early heart attack because of the wedding worries." Alex looked up at Nicholas, who was currently in the midst of pulling baking ingredients from the cabinets. He turned, looking back at him, a sad, stricken expression on his face. *Right.* Alex knew he was kind of being a jerk, throwing all his complaints at Nicholas at once. "I'm sorry. I don't mean it. I want to marry you, and I want to do it in the biggest, grandest, craziest wedding on the planet."

Nicholas looked at him, staring him down. He put the chocolate chips back. "You don't mean it. You don't want that kind of wedding. You can't make that any clearer if you try."

"I do!" Alex insisted. "I do. I want that."

"No! You've been saying this the whole time. You said you wanted to elope two days after we got engaged, and you're saying it now. Every single time we talk about the wedding, about anything bigger and grander than running to the courthouse, you get panicked about how it's too much for you!" Nicholas sighed, walking toward the printer, still buzzing out pages, this time, of a whole wedding planner that probably overlapped what Nicholas had already copied into his notebook. Without any warning, he pulled the plug out of the wall. "Okay. If that's what you want, a courthouse wedding, fine. We'll skip the big production."

Alex could hear the defeat in Nicholas's voice. He knew he was trying to be reasonable here, but he also knew he'd been planning his dream wedding since he was a teen, thinking it out with his mother and starting that binder he'd treasure forever. Aside from their engagement itself, Alex had rarely seen a sparkle in his eyes like the one where he got excited enough to pull out the binder and show it to him, to get it out of his storage boxes and flip through the pages, pointing out all the details and options. Alex remembered having a headache that night, but Nicholas's whole face lit up talking about all the possibilities. Alex was acutely aware that this situation was probably breaking Nicholas's heart.

Ultimately, Alex wanted to marry Nicholas. Of course, he did. But when it came to the how and the why, that's where he got stuck. How could two people, compatible in so many ways, have such a chasm between them on something that mattered so much, at least to one of them?

"No," Alex told him. He buried his face in his hands. "Nicholas, no. We're not going to call off the big, beautiful wedding of your dreams for a courthouse wedding." He was trying his hardest to make peace here.

"I just don't understand why you want a small wedding so badly," Nicholas admitted. "I mean, I love you. Part of that love is wanting to show you off to the world. I want our friends and our family and people driving down the side of the road to say, 'Holy crap, they love each other,' because they see our celebration and realize how wrapped up in each other we are."

Alex nodded and tried to take it in. "I get that, Nicholas," he said, using the calmest tone he could muster.

"And I get that you see weddings as disposable and pointless, an event to get over and done with so you can get on with the marriage itself. I've heard all the criticisms about waste and excess, not only from you but from everybody. Don't think I don't hear it from Veronica too. But I only plan on having one. One wedding in my whole life, one with you. So yeah, I want to make that a big deal."

"I know. I only want one too," Alex said. "But our love is so intense and strong that I don't think we have to make this a big spectacle. People know how we feel about one another when they see us together." He sighed and looked at Nicholas again, trying to read the expression on his face. "More than anything, though? I want you to be happy. Please, please get the flowers. All of them. Get a thousand of them and we'll figure it out." He tried hard to prove this was what he wanted, but Nicholas's sullen expression didn't change.

"Not if that's not what you want," Nicholas said, walking to the bedroom. "I just... Excuse me. I need a minute." Just before Nicholas got the door fully closed between them, Alex saw the look on his face, the one Nicholas got every time he had a good, hard cry. *Crap.*

*

Alex felt like a jerk. "Nicholas," he said, but the door stayed closed. He looked at the binder, holding the page open so the glue wouldn't make it stick and flipping through to the list at the front.

He scrawled a few tasks on a piece of paper:

> *Choose a theme*
>
> *Decide on Officiant*
>
> *Research Venues*
>
> *Register for Gifts*
>
> *Choose Honeymoon Location*
>
> *Decide on Wedding Rings*

He looked it over. That was a lot to do in one weekend, but he needed Nicholas to know he was serious about this.

> *The wedding of your dreams is the wedding of mine.*
>
> *Please come plan the wedding of our dreams together? I think we can tackle these things this weekend.*
>
> *I love you.*

He slipped the list under the bedroom door and sat down at the table, staring at the printer before plugging it back in. Within seconds, it whirred back to life and resumed the print job. He hoped that would be enough to convince Nicholas to come out and talk to him, that it would be enough to say he was in this. After all, he'd never meant to imply he wasn't, but the idea of them fighting about their wedding was the worst-case scenario.

He loved Nicholas. More than anything, he loved him, and if an extravagant wedding was the best way to prove it, he'd never mention eloping again.

A moment later, the bedroom door opened. "Really? All of this?" Nicholas quirked a brow up and walked to the table, where he crossed off a couple of items. "That's better. We can't even decide on a venue until we decide our theme. A modern wedding at the farmhouse of a winery? It would be a disaster." He smiled, eyes softer now.

Alex stood up. "Of course. We could never. What kind of classless gays would people think we were?" He wrapped his arms around Nicholas. "Forgive me?"

"If you'll forgive me," Nicholas answered, kissing Alex's hair. "Let's start with the registry. That's the fun part."

Chapter Seven

The Fun Part

It turned out Nicholas was right. Registering was the fun part of the whole equation. Alex held the scanner gun. "Pots and pans?" he asked.

"Are you kidding? Like I'd register for something new when I have my mother's!"

"Of course. No pots and pans. We pretty much have everything... What's there to register for?"

"The fun stuff. Gift cards so we can go out to eat when school and married life gets stressful. Matching bathrobes and slippers. Mouthwash because your breath is disgusting in the mornings and 'bad breath' isn't a valid reason for divorcing someone in a court of law," Nicholas joked.

"No, I mean, I think it is. I think my bad breath and your weirdly shaped toenails you can't seem to clip without my help could be filed under 'irreconcilable differences,'" Alex teased. Nicholas stuck his tongue out in response. "How about those albums we wanted to complete our collection?"

"Definitely those." Nicholas pivoted toward the music section without any additional warning.

Alex followed behind, scanner gun at the ready, stopping when he saw a set of picture frames. He scanned them without asking, saying, "We'll need these for the wedding photos." Picking the gifts they might receive was fun, especially knowing that their friends would know them better than they knew themselves, picking the appropriate gifts out from the list, or adding their own twist. He could easily assume Jade and Veronica would skip the registry altogether, go off-book and bring something fun and quirky. Brandon and Olivia would carefully go through the list and choose exactly the right gift. His grandparents, well...they probably wouldn't buy anything. He hadn't gotten up the nerve to tell them he was marrying a man. His mother's tone had shifted since the engagement, away from the strained but supportive tone she'd taken when he came out, to a new, more hesitant support. Either way, she'd probably focus on useful items, like towels. Speaking of... "What if we registered for bathroom stuff and did a little makeover in there? It could use an update."

Nicholas smiled. "Yeah, definitely. What's the plan? Got a color scheme in mind?"

"If I did, we wouldn't still have to decide a color scheme for our wedding. I'm bad with color decisions." Alex shrugged and turned down the bathroom aisle, which they were passing on their way back to the albums. "What do you think?"

Nicholas wasn't listening. Alex could tell by his body language, because he was already drawn to a specific shower curtain on display, holding on to the end and extending it out toward them both. The shower curtain was bold and modern, with stylish color blocking in soft pinks and pale greens, gray accents, and pops of black to contrast the pastels. Everything about the large piece of fabric was gorgeous.

Alex sidled up and elbowed Nicholas in the ribs. "Earth to Nicholas."

"Yeah?"

"You *do* remember we don't need a shower curtain, right? Glass shower door?" He waved a hand in front of his face.

"The colors, Alex. Look." Nicholas's voice was mesmerized and fascinated, drawn in by the color scheme.

"So...you want me to go grab towels and match them to this?" Alex asked, quirking his head to one side and glancing back and forth between Nicholas's eyes and the shower curtain.

"No, I...what about this for our wedding?" Nicholas kept holding it out. "We could get tuxes in this grey color, and then one of us could have this green for his vest and tie, and the other could wear the pinkish color..." He sounded wistful, focused.

"I'm assuming you've got dibs on the pink?"

Nicholas shrugged and kept staring. He was completely drawn in. Alex was okay with that, grabbing one of the wrapped shower curtains and putting it into the otherwise empty cart. They hadn't planned on shopping, focused on registering, but they'd gotten the cart just in case.

"We don't need to buy it," Nicholas said softly.

"Yeah, we do." Alex rubbed his back. "We'll need to color match it for the wedding, and then we can hold on to it and make it the first thing we put up in our home one day." If that didn't tell Nicholas he was on board with the wedding, he wasn't sure what would.

Nicholas turned to him in the aisle, tears in his eyes, and rested his arms loosely on his shoulders. "I love you."

Alex smiled and wiped his tears, kissing him in the middle of the bathroom section of the store. "I love you. I want us to have a beautiful wedding. Even if it is an adjustment for me, I want that." He needed Nicholas to know that much.

Nicholas smiled, and then his nose twitched, and before he could cover his mouth and pull away, he sneezed.

Chapter Eight

A Taste of His Own Medicine

Alex was getting a taste of his own medicine. Of course, this was bound to happen. He'd already told Nicholas he was contagious, sure Nicholas would catch his cold. And now Nicholas had. As Alex rubbed his back and made him tea, Nicholas continued to sneeze and cough, eyes dripping and nose running. "This sucks."

"Yeah," Alex said. "It's miserable. Do you want me to get a honey bear from Jade?"

Nicholas shook his head. "I don't think it's allergies."

"I *told* you," Alex laughed. "Why don't you go back to sleep?" Nicholas nodded and laid down, pulling the blankets up past his ears, blowing his nose and generally looking miserable.

Alex had no choice but to do what Nicholas had done for him. For weeks, Nicholas had dutifully tended to his needs, running him hot showers with eucalyptus and bringing him tea and making him dinners that would cure him. Alex could do most of those things, but the dinners eluded him.

In the kitchen, he flipped through the recipe box looking for any soup he could manage properly, finding the chicken and dumplings Nicholas swore by. They didn't look *too* complicated. Boiling the chicken was one part, then...the rest of it. He bit his lip and pondered. Could he actually pull it off? He wasn't entirely sure. He didn't really have a choice though. Nicholas needed this to recover, and Alex was determined to try. He put the recipe box back on the refrigerator and studied the recipe he'd pulled out. "Starting easy. Boil the chicken," he said to himself, door closed between him and Nicholas so he wouldn't disturb his sleep. Thankfully, Nicholas was at least sneezing less than he was the past four days since they'd been to the store to register.

Alex pulled chicken breasts from the freezer and put them in the pot. "Okay, it...doesn't say how much water to use." He bit his lip and considered it, eventually filling the pot enough to cover the chicken. He added bay leaves because the recipe said so—even though they didn't taste like anything, as far as he could tell—and onions because that's what Nicholas's mother had always done. Then he dropped in the stick of butter. It melted in the boiling liquid. "Now what? I just wait until this stuff cooks?" He quirked an eyebrow and then shrugged. "Guess I've got time to work then."

He was almost halfway through his thesis, and if he could have a good half hour of work time, it would help him make progress. As he sat down by his computer, he glanced at the pot. "What's that saying? A watched pot never boils?" Nicholas had said that again and again, usually to justify getting it on while waiting for water to boil for pasta or rice or any number of dishes, or at least for a quick make out session. And a few times, a game of

Go Fish. Alex chuckled to himself and focused on the screen, pulling up research and typing notes in his open document. His eyes flicked back and forth between halves of his screen, then between tabs in the window as he worked. An hour passed. Then half of another.

The crackling sound caught his attention before anything else did. "Oh shoot!" He added the last two words of his sentence as he heard the *whoosh,* which got more of his attention. Glancing toward the stove as he stood, he startled at the sight in front of him. That was when he smelled it. His nose hadn't been working as well since he was sick, but the scent of fire was unmistakable. Or maybe he imagined he smelled it, brain connecting wires his nose didn't. He didn't have time to think. He could only rush to action, and as he raced closer to the fire, the flames that had started on the stove already licked at the cabinets and spread rapidly across the counters. His heart raced as he watched them consume the canisters in which they stored the kitchen goods they used most frequently. Alex raced toward the fire and pulled the recipe box down to clutch it to his chest. If he only had time to save one item in the kitchen, he had to save the recipes. They were Nicholas's most prized possession, a treasured hand-me-down through generations.

The box was small and wooden, one his great-grandfather had made and his grandmother had decorated. The importance of the recipes, and so many other items, flitted through Alex's mind as he kept the box safe against his body, the heat of the blaze singeing the hair on his arms, stinging the skin as he yanked himself away from the fire and raced to the bedroom.

"Nicholas!" he screamed, shoving the recipes at him. "Take these and go!" He raced back into the kitchen.

Months before, Alex had burned macaroni so badly it set the smoke alarms off in their apartment, smoke alarms that were screeching loudly now as the flames lapped at the ceiling. They'd joked about getting a fire extinguisher before, but neither of them had ever bothered. Now, there was no way to stop the blaze in front of him. Helplessness overwhelmed Alex. The flames were too big to smother, so he turned on the sink faucet, aiming the sprayer toward the fire. The water only made it pop and sizzle, then grow hotter. "Dammit!" he screamed, pulling away as the blaze got stronger and more intense.

He raced back to the bedroom. "Nicholas, there's a fire in the kitchen!" Ordinarily, the fire alarms would have been more than enough to make that clear, but Nicholas had been mostly asleep and was sick. Information didn't connect as easily, and Alex knew that all too well. "We have to go!"

Getting Nicholas into gear was hard. He knew too well the fog that came with the cold he'd had, the delay between information and processing it, but this was life or death. He needed Nicholas to get up, to get out, and to go, and he could see the second Nicholas processed the situation properly, body jerking to action, even as he looked bleary-eyed and dazed.

Even as he ran into the living room, the flames creeping along the ceiling and air thick, he worried that they'd get out in time, or get anyone else in the building out in time. He had to pull Nicholas back more than once, begging him not to go for special priceless items, things they both wanted to save. Alex knew the significance; there was just no time. His mind raced with what they needed to do, as they crawled to the door until they heard a loud bang. "Oh my god!" Alex yelped. They had to find another way out, not through the half wall past the kitchen to the entrance. There had to be another option. "Let's go to the balcony instead."

The idea was risky. Alex knew there wasn't a fire escape ladder on the balcony; it had long rusted, and no one had ever replaced it. But the balcony was better than breathing in toxic air, so he crawled into the other direction and opened the glass door, giving Nicholas a chance to follow him out.

Alex gasped for fresh air, something that smelled better than the burnt smoke-filled air inside. Nicholas reached for him and rubbed his back with one hand, clinging to the box of recipes as if his life depended on it with the other. "We have to call 9-1-1." As Alex started to dial, Nicholas said, "Oh no! We forgot—"

They forgot too many things, so many that mattered to Nicholas personally, and to Alex, and to their relationship together. "Nicholas, we can't go back in," Alex told him. "Whatever we're forgetting, it's not as important as us being outside, okay?" And that was true, nothing mattered more than the fact that he and Nicholas were both alive, even if they lost everything inside. Nicholas nodded and teared up, but they were stuck; there was no way to save their belongings. Whatever had been lost in the blaze, they'd worry about it after.

Alex pulled his phone from his pocket. There were too many people inside the building and only so long the fireproofing would hold out. He texted Jade first.

ALEX: *Pull the fire alarm.*

JADE: *Why?*

It made sense she'd ask. On the opposite side of the building, she wouldn't have smelled or seen the fire yet. But her help could save lives, or at least get people out of the building faster.

ALEX: *Kitchen fire. Calling 9-1-1*

He didn't have time to wait for a response, because he needed to get more help than that. He dialed and waited, listening and hoping for the dispatcher to pick up. For some reason, it felt like it took forever. It had only been a couple of rings. Every second he waited for them to answer was one more second the flames destroyed their apartment, their memories within, the essence of their lives. He couldn't control the obvious sadness in his voice, the choked-up desperation as he told the dispatcher what was happening. As he spoke, the fire alarms blared inside. Jade had listened to him, thankfully. Maybe adequate warning would protect everyone else, give them the chance to get out faster. As he explained their location and the nature of the fire to the woman on the other end of the line, the flames licked at the edges of a picture they'd hung on the wall right after their engagement, a cute snapshot Jade had taken of them sharing an ice cream cone from a local shop. Tears streamed down Alex's face as he watched it blacken and melt.

From the balcony, Alex couldn't feel the heat. Somehow still, he imagined he could as he watched it, glancing down at the singed hair on his arm. He kept talking to the person on the end of the line, heart racing. He turned away from the apartment and looked down at the ground below. People filtered from the front doors of the apartment building, turning to look and pointing up at the apartment above them.

Nicholas, clearly fully awake now, turned toward Alex. "What the heck happened?" he mused as Alex hung up the phone. The fire trucks were on the scene now. A tanker was already backing up to get them off the balcony, ladder starting to extend.

"I was trying to make you soup," Alex said. The reality of the situation began to sink in. Guilt cut through every other thought he had. "I'm so sorry." The fire was his fault. He'd gotten so distracted working on his thesis that he'd forgotten to check on the chicken on the stove, and his lingering congestion had made it hard for him to smell it burning until it was too late. Alex burst into a sob, and Nicholas wrapped his free arm around Alex to comfort him, letting him bury his face against his neck.

From there, Alex didn't have to face the fire, and as the firefighter came up to help them both down, Alex tried to resist the urge to look through the window. He didn't want to know. He couldn't handle knowing. He turned toward them and waited for instructions, making the climb down. As he did, going first at their advice because he was closer, he said, "I'm sorry," again. Not that it changed anything. The crackle of the fire was audible from outside the building now, and their lives were going up in smoke.

*

Nicholas had yet to process what was happening. He sat on the back of a fire truck, a mylar blanket draped over his shoulders and his prized recipes in hand. He knew they represented a multitude of baking and cooking equipment that would be ruined in the blaze, among other parts of his family history he'd inherited. "This isn't your fault," he said, reaching forward to take Alex's hand. "This isn't on you."

Alex nodded but Nicholas could see the hesitation in his eyes. "It *is* my fault. I knew I wasn't a good cook. I knew better than to try to make one of those complicated recipes. I should have stuck with canned soup. I probably would have found a way to burn the kitchen down even without overcomplicating things."

"Sweetheart, it happens. Accidents happen." Nicholas smoothed his thumb over Alex's hand. He understood. If the roles had been reversed, he would have been blaming himself. "I'm sure we'll be able to salvage some stuff, and we'll probably be able to stay in another unit until it gets sorted out."

Alex nodded again, looking at his feet.

"You were trying to make me feel better. You did good," Nicholas told him. Nothing Nicholas said was likely to help. Nicholas knew better than to think it would. But he still needed to try. He needed Alex to understand he wasn't upset; he knew Alex had only tried to help. "Come on, let's go talk to Jade."

Finding Jade wasn't hard. She was on the other side of the truck, talking to one of the firefighters. The part Nicholas wasn't ready to hear was what he was telling her, the part where he called it a "total loss." He stepped closer.

"Seriously? Nothing made it?"

The firefighter's eyes widened. Nicholas imagined he wasn't supposed to be sharing information like that with her before he'd told Nicholas himself. But he just shrugged. "I'm sorry, sir. Between the fire damage and the smoke damage and then the water damage of putting it out...it'll be a shock if much is left after this."

Alex gasped from behind Nicholas. Nicholas had assumed *something* would be salvageable, and apparently, Alex had too. "When can we go see it?" Alex asked.

"You'll have to give it a few days. Call your renter's insurance. I'm sure they'll put you up in a hotel for the night, or you guys will need to book one, make sure the hotspots are all gone, and we'll get out of there, and then you can come back with an officer and pick through what's left. You'll need one of us with you to make sure that there's no danger. Fires make floorboards weak and can cause roof collapses." He looked back up at the building and then at Nicholas and Alex again. "The building has excellent fireproofing, but your upstairs and downstairs neighbors, and those to each side of you, are going to be displaced too. You're not alone in this."

Alex cried harder as Nicholas wrapped his arms around him. "I know. It's okay." Nicholas felt numb. The shock of it hadn't hit him yet and he knew that. Perhaps it was because Alex had seen the whole blaze from the beginning. Nicholas hadn't had time to deal with it yet. Jade wrapped them both in her arms, hugging them the best she could, and Nicholas appreciated that. A group hug wouldn't fix the pain, but it couldn't hurt.

"If you need to stay with us until you can get back in the apartment, go for it. I'm sure Veronica won't mind," Jade told them, voice muffled against Nicholas's arm from her much shorter stature.

"Thanks," Nicholas said. "We might take you up on that tomorrow. I think a hotel is probably a good idea for tonight so we can do some shopping." He looked down at himself, not wearing shoes.

Chapter Nine

Aftershock

Smoke. Alex could breathe enough to smell the remnants of smoke. But it wasn't only that. There was a weird damp smell, like a wet dog—sans the dog—plus all their paint and plastics and furniture. As he crossed the threshold and looked around, he couldn't wrap his brain around how different their home looked.

"Whoa," Nicholas said. Whoa was right. Nothing in the place appeared normal. Their gray apartment walls were much darker now, licked with flames that left behind streaks of black soot. Alex smudged his finger across one. In some places, it revealed the brighter gray underneath, but mostly, the surface stayed charred.

In the kitchen, their backsplash was melted, a stick-on plastic Nicholas had added to set their apartment apart from the base features offered by university housing. They'd intended to peel it off when they moved, add a little Goo Gone, and call it good. Now, the shell of their little upgrade remained, stuck to the wall forever in a chaotic burnt mess. Nicholas lifted his phone to photograph some of the damage, dodging the water that dripped from the ceiling.

Alex tried stepping over debris, walking closer to the source of the fire. That was where most of the damage remained. The cabinets above the fridge had been incinerated, and the one above the stove was almost entirely gone. Doors hung and listed on other cabinets, no longer neat and tidy like before. Even the one that had been constantly, ever-so-slightly open because of the serving platter that didn't quite fit was burned open forever, and if they touched it, it would probably fall apart.

Looking around, Alex was tired. Not only from lack of sleep—though that played a factor, because although the hotel was nice, he hadn't been in the correct frame of mind to appreciate it—but from the ache of losing everything. They'd replaced the essentials at the store the night before: toothbrushes, a couple of changes of clothes, shoes for Nicholas. They'd have to go get more, but what was the point in spending that kind of money until they heard from the insurance company? All night long, he'd struggled to shut the images out of his mind. Every time he closed his eyes, no matter how tired he was, he saw the images of orange-yellow flames, sensed the heat and the smoke, and sat up panting and panicked. Nicholas had tried to comfort him, but the cold medicine made him tired, not that it helped the ragged cough any.

He couldn't stop thinking about it, about what they'd lost. Every album he'd ever bought. Nicholas's family heirlooms. Hell, the shower curtain they'd decided to fashion their wedding after. All of it was gone, solely because he wasn't a good cook.

And not just things, items he could hold or touch, but safety. That apartment had been the first real safe place he'd lived. His mother's home had been technically safe, but he never felt like he could open up and be himself there—too many of his memories were tinged with sadness or anxiety. His own apartment across the hall had helped, but nothing had made him feel safe the way this shared apartment did. And now their safe space was gone, the home where he was truly himself for the first time ripped away.

Nicholas looked above Alex's head as he stood near the fridge and he wrapped his arms around Alex. "See? You saved the recipes. They'd have been a complete loss."

Alex shrugged. "All of your cookbooks..." he said softly. He looked at Nicholas, went to the lower cabinet they were in, and opened it. Exactly as he'd suspected, almost all of them had been destroyed by fire or water.

Nicholas reached past him and pulled out a couple that were partially damaged, but not fully. "A few made it." He made a small stack of them outside the front door, a fraction of the total cookbooks he owned. Alex figured some books were better than none, but Nicholas had collected those for years, and then his family for decades before.

Alex studied the living room, seeing his warped laptop on the table and the printer that was melted to the charred table beneath it. He walked over and touched it, watching as the worst leg of the table crumbled and left it leaning. He tried not to cry. Picking up a spiral spring, he frowned. Gobs of notes, all taken in earnest to incorporate into projects, and none of them backed up online...gone. He'd lost countless hours of work in the span of a few minutes.

"Alex, look!" Nicholas yelped, and Alex ran over.

"What?"

"My cast iron!" He pulled it out and showed Alex. The cookware was dark, but it had withstood the test of the flame. Relief washed over him. If nothing else, the heirloom pieces survived the fire in a way the rest of the cookware—more recently purchased, all nonstick—had not.

"Thank goodness," Alex said. He scanned the rest of the cabinets, opening doors and watching them fall apart under his touch in hopes that something else might have survived. Nicholas looked around, a puzzled expression on his face. "What are you looking for?" Alex asked.

"The, um, the binder," Nicholas said.

"Where was it?"

For a long while, Nicholas's brow furrowed in thought. Alex was pretty sure he'd left the book by the printer, but then Nicholas let out a soft sound of frustration. "Oh." They'd been looking at it in the kitchen, where the fire had started. He rushed over there and reached the counter. A single metal spiral stayed on the cabinet, a few remnants of the cover melted to the wood beneath. The binder was a total loss. "It's gone," Nicholas said, choking on a sob as he made a beeline for the front door, sank to the ground, and cried into his hands as Alex followed behind helplessly.

"I'm sorry," Alex said. "I'm so, so sorry." No apology could be good enough. Not when Nicholas had spent more than a decade working on the planner. Not when his mother had put as much tender care into it as Nicholas had. There was no replacing the binder because the binder had never only been about the wedding.

"It's fine," Nicholas said, his tone taking on an icy chill. "It wasn't the wedding you wanted anyway."

*

Nicholas tried his hardest to pretend like he wasn't mad. Logically, he knew the fire was an accident. Alex had tried to do something nice, and he hadn't ever intended for the kind act to incinerate the binder. But logic didn't factor into his emotions, and emotionally, he'd lost the strongest tie he had to his mother. Despite spending a week trying to get over the loss, his heart still ached. As much as Nicholas tried not to believe the fire was malicious—because *of course* he knew Alex hadn't set the place on fire purposefully—he couldn't help feeling like Alex hadn't wanted the perfect wedding or the binder in the first place, so he could never understand the grief Nicholas was experiencing. Why save the recipes, which had been scanned in and backed up, and not the binder instead? Jade's words about backing that up haunted him, even though he knew a scanned version of the binder wouldn't have been the same in the first place.

Alex was trying. Consciously, Nicholas knew that. Alex had tended to his every need and waited on him hand and foot, trying to get them moved into their new apartment and settled carefully while Nicholas rested from being sick. The thing was, Nicholas didn't feel sick anymore anyway. He was just...sad.

They'd both lost treasured belongings in the fire. Alex had lost photo albums and letters from his mom from the past year, the clothes he'd had sitting in a laundry basket on the couch waiting to be folded, his laptop, his school notes, so many items. But Nicholas had lost almost every project he and his mother had made together, stuff he'd saved to remember her by, every treasured letter from his family, and many family photographs. Some were online, of course, and a few were spared from fire and water damage, but many weren't backed up at all. There were irreplaceable memories in that apartment for both of them, but no loss stung the way the binder did.

Nicholas cried. He cried in ways he hadn't for years, taking overly long showers to get the tears out so Alex wouldn't see. He tried to keep quiet and not make a show of it. The last thing he needed was for Alex to feel more guilt than he already did. But the undercurrent of anger was there, as much as Nicholas didn't want for it to be present. No matter how hard he tried, he was still hurt. Sad, but angry. He'd consider this part of the stages of grief, but when it came to losing his mother, father, and aunt, he'd never really followed those stages cohesively. This time, he skipped straight to anger, if this counted as grief.

He had so many questions. Why hadn't Alex gone for the canned soup like he'd mentioned? And why had Alex tried to cook for him in the first place? He pushed those thoughts aside and told himself Alex was trying to help. He was an attentive fiancé, caring and kind, and Nicholas usually loved that about him. Now, it got under his skin. Not because he wanted Alex to be different, not really, but because he wanted their entire lives back. And as hard as he wanted to try not to blame Alex, as much as he didn't blame him entirely, he bristled with annoyance. And that came with guilt too. Maybe not to the same caliber of guilt Alex held, but a certain level of guilt knowing Alex had only ever tried to help. It just hadn't been...helpful.

"So, I was thinking we could buy that shower curtain again. I mean, we need one now anyway, don't we?" Alex asked. Moving apartments had meant moving buildings entirely, since the one they'd been living in was completely full.

"Yeah. Sure." Nicholas picked at the mushroom noodle bake their friend, Brandon's girlfriend, Olivia, had brought them. The dish tasted good enough, but Nicholas's mind wasn't on eating. He focused on the wedding and what they'd lost.

"Sure? That's all? Just...sure?" Alex quirked an eyebrow at him.

Nicholas put his fork down and glared across the table. "Sure. We can buy the shower curtain."

"What's wrong?" Alex asked him. As if Alex didn't know. As if Alex wasn't sure what was wrong—the many, many things that were wrong.

"I just don't see any reason to keep with that plan for the wedding when it isn't the wedding you want," Nicholas snapped. He knew he was being unreasonable. He knew this wasn't fair to Alex. He knew Alex was on board with the shower curtain color scheme too. But reason wasn't at the forefront of his mind.

"Is that what this is? The long showers and the angry slamming around and the cold shoulder you've been giving me for days?"

"No!" Nicholas shot back. *Yes*. "It's about the whole situation. I mean, I knew you hated the wedding, but seriously? My wedding binder is just...gone!"

"Nicholas, I couldn't... I couldn't save the binder and the recipes. The counter was already on fire. I burned the hair off my arm trying to get the recipes and the fire wasn't even to the fridge yet!" Alex teared up and Nicholas instantly felt bad.

"I know." Nicholas looked away and picked up his fork again. "I know. You didn't mean for it to happen, and you did an amazing job saving our stuff. I'm sorry."

"Nicholas, if you knew that, if you really believed the fire wasn't malicious, you wouldn't have said it," Alex explained. "I promise you I wasn't trying to sabotage your plan for the wedding. Say I had a problem with the wedding—which I swear to you, I don't—I know what that binder meant to you outside of our plans. I wouldn't have let that get ruined if I could have helped it." Alex sighed and stood up. He pushed his chair in. "I think I'm going to go to bed."

Alex never left an argument early. Never. They worked hard to communicate through their anger and not walk away from it. The fact that he felt he needed to now spoke volumes to Nicholas. "Alex, wait."

Alex froze in place. "Yeah?"

"I love you. I know it wasn't on purpose," he repeated. "I'm sorry."

"Thanks. I'm sorry too." He sat back down in his chair. "But you still think I don't want the wedding to be this big celebration, and it breaks my heart because I'm not sure how to make it clear to you that I'm okay with it."

"The fact that you're only *okay* with it is the problem." He shook his head, stung by Alex's remark. "The fact that I'm planning a wedding, thinking I can make sure it makes us both happy, and you've decided it's...suitable. Tolerable, maybe. That's what I'm frustrated about."

"Nicholas, I didn't mean—"

"Yeah, Alex. I know. But I think you did, actually. Subconsciously even. I'll come up with a new plan. I'll start over." He buried his face in his hands, rubbing at it. "I'll try harder."

Nicholas wasn't sure what was more devastating to him: the fire, the binder, or the thought that Alex was this unhappy and hadn't said a single word since starting to pretend he was on board.

Chapter Ten

Making it Right

Alex knocked on Jade's door with one hand, holding a large sack in the other hand. He glanced down at the bag as he waited, willing it not to bust through the rest of the way. The sack was overstuffed, corners of magazines poking through.

"Alex," Veronica said, swinging open the door.

"Hey, V."

"What's up?" She took a step back, gesturing to let him in.

"I need a favor from you and Jade." Veronica was great, but he mostly needed Jade's help here. V, much like himself, was not much of a sentimental person. Jade, though, she'd get what he needed.

"Yeah, of course. Come on in. You don't have to stand in the entry." Veronica smiled and led him in farther. "What's in the sack?"

"I'm getting to that," Alex said quietly. He was a little nervous Jade would think this was the dumbest idea on the planet. He came in and set his bag near the door, looking for Jade, who stood at the stove, stirring some kind of dinner that smelled absolutely divine.

"Hey!" Jade looked up from what she was mixing with a wide grin. "You came at the right time. I was about to package up half of this chicken spaghetti so I could bring it to you and Nicky." She turned back to the stove. "What brings you to our side of town? Still grabbing stuff from the old place?"

Alex shook his head. "No. There's nothing left there." He walked in and leaned against the kitchen island. "I actually came to ask a favor."

"What's that?" Jade asked.

He looked back and forth between the two of them. "I'm trying to fix what I ruined. Nicholas thinks I hate his ideas for the wedding because I let the binder get ruined. Or that's not *why,* but it's kind of why? Because I said I was okay with the wedding."

"Oh, shit. You didn't say it in those words, did you?" Jade asked.

"What words? That I was okay with it? Unfortunately, yes."

Even Veronica winced. "Oof. That's...oof. I would have made the same mistake, and Jade would have probably skinned me alive."

"Which brings me here." He looked at his sack on the floor by the door. "Listen, I bought some wedding magazines, and a binder, and the shower curtain, and uh... I was wondering if I could stash it at your place so he wouldn't find it until I was done?"

"Shower curtain?" Veronica asked.

"They picked their wedding colors because Nicholas fell in love with a shower curtain. Keep up, V," Jade joked, sliding a baking dish into the oven. "Okay, so...you're what, collecting supplies so he can make a new one?"

"No. I, uh, I thought if I tried to remake it...or not remake it, exactly. I can't bring back what he and his mom made together," he said, admitting that nothing he did would bring back what the binder meant. "I thought if I made *a* wedding binder, he would understand I really love his wedding ideas." He glanced at the sack. "I bought all of his favorite wedding magazines at the store." He couldn't make it up to Nicholas, not fully, because in reality, nothing could replace what he'd lost. Alex had never seen Nicholas this inconsolable before, and he understood the pain. Alex couldn't bring back his mother and the time they invested and the energy and love they'd put into caring for Nicholas's wedding binder during the last couple of years of her life. They'd worked on it as a chemo distraction, spent time talking about an event she would never be there to see. Alex couldn't fix that. But he could show he cared, or that he was trying.

Veronica looked at him and blinked. "Would that make him more upset? Here's a binder but it's not *your* binder?" It didn't sound accusatory, but Alex did wish he had given her the opportunity to say that before he'd spent an ungodly amount of money on materials for it. He looked at the floor as Jade wrapped her arms around his own in a small side-hug.

"No. It won't. Because you know Nicholas is going to see what Alex is trying to do, and he's going to be thankful for his thoughtfulness." She said it pointedly, raising an eyebrow, and Alex appreciated her coming to his defense there.

Alex nodded. "I just figured if I kept it here and tucked it away, he wouldn't find it until I was done." He smiled. "I'll pick it up tomorrow so I can go work on it at the coffee shop, or whatever, and try to get it finished as fast as I can."

Jade picked a couple of the magazines out of the bag. "Do you want help? You're welcome to work on it here instead, and I can help you with whatever you need."

Veronica was in agreement this time, nodding. "You're welcome here anytime, Alex. No need to go to a coffee shop unless you want to. You spend enough time there as it is."

"Thanks, guys. Seriously. You're right. By the time my shift's over... I'd rather do it here." He smiled and squeezed Veronica's hand. "Do you need help with that?" he asked Jade, nodding toward the cake mix she was stirring.

Jade smirked. "No offense, Alex, but I think I'll handle any meals that require the use of heat."

Alex nodded and forced a laugh, trying to ignore the sinking feeling he had. The joke she made was good—and warranted—and he knew she teased him in good spirit, but the comment ripped open the wound. He wouldn't trust himself around heat either.

Before he could ask if Jade wanted him to take the food to Nicholas, she smiled and said, "I'll take the chicken spaghetti over in an hour, so Nicholas has no idea you were here conspiring."

Alex hugged her. "Thanks, Jade." He had amazing friends, and he was a little heartbroken they weren't neighbors anymore. That may have been the biggest loss from the fire.

*

Nicholas wondered what was taking Alex so long to get home from work. After his dream internship fell through, he'd found work at a coffee shop. The job wasn't Alex's first pick, especially because it didn't tie in to his major and wasn't exactly a resume booster, but it brought in some income and gave Alex a sense of purpose. Work, Nicholas knew, was deep in Alex's bones, something he insisted on doing, even if Nicholas reminded him, he could focus on school and not worry about a job right now. But Alex lamented many times that he didn't want to use Nicholas's inheritance or let his teaching fellowship pay for their rent. So, Nicholas didn't protest as they split bills down the middle, as much as he wanted to argue. Alex kept saying it would come in handy if Nicholas needed a break between his teaching fellowship and finding a job, but Nicholas was determined not to need that. He'd been applying to a lot of great positions. Alex didn't need to be concerned about money or put his focus on working so Nicholas wouldn't have to.

Now, though, Alex was an hour and a half late after his shift. Nicholas tried not to worry. He could have stayed late to study or had a study group he hadn't mentioned. Maybe he'd gone to the library or met with someone to replace notes lost in the fire. Trying not to worry, and not worrying, were different things entirely, mostly because Alex rarely stayed late without a text letting Nicholas know. He wondered if their argument the other day was still weighing on him. That only added guilt to his worry. "Alex, where the heck are you?" he mumbled to himself. As if on cue, Alex walked in, visor in his hand and face looking worn and weary. "Long day?"

"The longest," Alex said, hanging his visor on the hook and walking over to give Nicholas a quick peck. "Feel like I haven't sat down in the past year and a half." He sank onto their couch, which whined in protest. The springs creaked, the couch time-worn and well-loved, a secondhand find at a spring garage sale. The fabric didn't match their exact aesthetic but replacing all the furniture they'd lost in the fire was out of the question while they were also spending a lot on the wedding. Again, at least in Alex's mind. Nicholas would have gladly dipped into his savings. The couch might have been ugly, but it worked. And Alex actually liked the couch, so that made it even better. Nicholas walked closer, seeing Alex's arm draped across his eyes.

"Sounds like you need a foot rub," he said, heading for the bedroom to grab lotion. He came back and pulled Alex's feet into his lap instead, and Alex sat up more. "You had a long day today. Thought you were off at five." Nicholas wasn't trying to accuse or pry. He was just worried. Alex had stressed about the fire until he got bags under his eyes from lack of sleep, and Nicholas feared how much he was letting it get to him. He pumped lotion into his hand and worked at the soreness in Alex's left foot, rubbing at the ball of it and smoothing lotion into the dry, cracked heels.

"I was supposed to be. Somebody showed up late."

Nicholas nodded and kept applying the lotion, rubbing it between Alex's toes, wriggling them until Alex giggled.

"Stop, I can't talk when you tickle me!" Alex protested, but he didn't pull away.

"That's the goal. Get you checked out of that head once in a while."

"That was the other part. Got off work, decided to go for a walk. Sorry I wasn't home sooner, I just... I needed time to think."

Nicholas frowned and furrowed his brow. "Why do you feel the need to apologize for that?" They both had their preferred ways of getting alone time. Before the fire, Alex had been obsessed with playing *Pro Skater 2* on an ancient system, but until the insurance got back with them about how much they'd pay out for the itemized list they gave, playing video games wasn't an option for him. Nicholas preferred hot showers and baking to clear his mind.

"I didn't tell you. I didn't text, I didn't call, I just... walked."

"Alex, you don't have to always text and call and tell me where you are." He worked his way to Alex's other foot. "I'm secure in this. I don't have to keep tabs on you."

Alex nodded, but Nicholas still felt like he was holding back. He knew the guilt Alex locked inside himself and the way he internalized it. His own outburst about the binder hadn't helped matters, but Nicholas was over it. Not over the binder, because he would never be able to recover the lost memories, but over his frustration and annoyance. Or he thought so at least. There was no point in stewing about a loss that couldn't be undone, especially one that was accidental in the first place.

As Nicholas rubbed his other foot, they fell into silence. Not the typical, comfortable silence they often had around each other, the one they'd share when Nicholas was grading papers or Alex was studying notes, nor the focused quiet of Nicholas baking while Alex worked on his thesis. Instead, they fell into the kind of uncomfortable stillness of words left unsaid, the feeling Alex wanted to say something, but wasn't saying it, and that Nicholas needed to say more but didn't know what. So, they sat, not speaking, with Nicholas rubbing Alex's feet and hoping the affectionate gesture said enough.

The knock at the door ten minutes later jerked Nicholas from his thoughts, and he nudged Alex's legs off his lap and headed for the door. "Jade!" he said, smiling and starting to wrap his arms around her before he saw she was carrying a foil baking pan. "What's this?"

"Chicken spaghetti." She glanced toward Alex and smiled before turning her attention to Nicholas. "I thought I'd bring you dinner."

The meals had been steady since the house fire. They had replaced some of their cookware, but not all of it, and while they could cook meals, their friends had insisted on showering them with love and bringing food instead. Nicholas was itching to get back in the kitchen again, but he appreciated the thought, smiling. "Are you joining us? We'd love to have you." He got three plates from the cabinet, some melamine ones they'd bought the other day.

"No. I made another batch, and V and I are going to eat that one. Thanks though." She leaned against the counter and studied Nicholas's face. "How are you doing?"

"I'm fine. I told you that earlier," he said. "Stop worrying so much. We're fine. Miss being there, but we're fine." Maybe he was protesting too much. The new building was ten minutes away, the closest vacant apartment to the university and their work. Living on campus, in the grad apartments, would have been more ideal, but it was better than nothing.

"The more you say fine, the less I'm inclined to believe you're actually fine," Jade said, a sympathetic smile budding on her face.

Nicholas hated the pitying looks from his friends, which is why he'd insisted he was fine, but he didn't have a good response to the constant concern that *fine* didn't mean fine. "Jade…" he said softly. "We just miss you." That was the easiest way to word it.

"We miss you too. I don't know what we'll do at Christmas if you aren't moved back there." She smiled and squeezed his arm gently. Nicholas hoped they'd be back then, too, because even though he no longer qualified for student housing, his fiancé had a year left of his program, and still had access to their old normal life in the graduate student apartments. "So, I have a plan. I wanted to tell you in person." She threw a glance at Alex, who put his socks back on and walked over.

"This smells good," Alex said.

"I know. It's delicious." She winked at him and then turned back to Nicholas. "You two never had an engagement party. That's a real problem. So…I want to change it and throw you two a little engagement bash. Okay?"

"Really?" Nicholas asked. His mind raced with ideas. They could have a garden party, an outdoor event in the beautiful spring weather. It could incorporate a bolder twist on their color scheme, bright and springtime, nodding at the ultimate wedding plan. He pictured little tea cakes and—

"Really. I'm going to plan it, and it'll be the perfect party, and all you two have to do is show up." She beamed and Nicholas forced a smile. He was endlessly thankful for Jade and genuinely excited to celebrate with her, but the thought of not having a hand in the party freaked him out. Jade was amazing, talented, and fun, but she could be scattered. A part of him worried that if she was keeping him out of the planning, it wouldn't actually go off perfectly like he hoped. She smirked at him then. "I can see the wheels turning in your head. Take a breath, Nicholas. You have more important issues to worry about than a party. You focus on you two being okay, and I'll focus on throwing you a great event."

Nicholas smiled again and nodded, pulling her into a hug. "Thank you. You are the best friend in the whole world." He tried to relax and let his worries subside. What Jade was offering was incredibly kind, something she didn't have to do, and Nicholas focused on that, the sense of thankfulness there. He'd have to find a way to keep his concerns to himself and let her work her magic.

Chapter Eleven

Micromanager

Jade's texts made her exasperation clear. Nicholas almost felt bad. Almost. But texting her wasn't giving him enough information, like whether she needed him to do anything for the party or not. He'd have been happy to pick up ingredients for recipes, or get tablecloths, or...whatever, really. But all he got in response from her was "everything's fine." Of course, she'd made it clear that fine didn't mean fine during their last conversation. So, he drove over there, singing along to his playlist the entire way. The fire might have taken his binder and all the tangible pieces of it, but it didn't take the wedding playlist they'd been curating for their entire relationship. Or Nicholas had been curating. Alex had no idea about his contributions to it, how Nicholas had taken all the songs that Alex had said reminded him of their relationship and added them to the list. To Nicholas, the playlist was a nice secret. Maybe someday he'd clue Alex in, give it to him as a gift, the way one might have swapped mix CDs in middle school. He'd never done that, but he had friends who did, and he thought it might be a sweet way of giving this to Alex. Later. Not now.

Alone in the car, Nicholas wasn't shy about belting the lyrics. Not that Alex ever minded him singing loudly anymore, and not that he stopped himself from doing so most times, but here, alone, his true passion for the songs shone, no self-consciousness present at all. He knew he wasn't great at singing, but he liked to pretend he was. If nothing else, this was a good warm-up for the next time the four of them ventured to a karaoke bar. As he pulled into his old apartment building, sadness crept over him. He pulled into the spot he used to always park in and looked up at the building. Any joy he had from singing was gone as he looked at the streaks of black soot on the brick exterior of his old home. "Just go in and focus on seeing Jade." If only telling himself that could take his mind off the ache in his chest. Even as he walked into the lobby, up the stairs, the pangs of familiarity struck him. How many times had he walked this path before? How many times had he roamed these halls caroling or hiding small Easter eggs with trinkets outside neighbors' doors? As he knocked on Jade's door, he resisted the urge to cry. Still, tears welled in his eyes.

Jade swung the door open and gave him a look, lips pursed. "I was just texting you back," she said, but then she must have seen the expression in his eyes, because immediately after, she wrapped her arms around him. "Come in. Talk to me. What's wrong?"

Nicholas followed her in but didn't talk. He knew saying it would only make his tears spill over. "I'm fine."

"You're not." She guided him toward the couch. "Sit. Talk."

"It's fine!" he insisted.

"Nicholas, I know you better than anyone on this planet, I'm telling you. You keep using that word again and again, but I *know* you. You're not fine. Is this because you're worried I'm going to botch your party?"

Nicholas shook his head and sniffled. "No. It's...I thought we could talk about it, and you could tell me if there's some way I can help with it, but coming here reminded me that I'm *not* here and I...shoot, Jade, I really miss it here."

She nodded and hugged him gently before sitting down in a chair opposite him. "I know. Has it gotten any easier?" she asked.

He shook his head. "Honestly, I thought it had. We're all settled in now, and I love it there. We have a bathtub!" They had always wanted a bathtub, and Jade knew his longing for the tub well, from trips to Lush where he'd smell every bubble bar in the store, coveting them and wishing he had a reason to buy them. But a bathtub wasn't enough to ease the loss. "I come back here and I just...lose it a little." He sighs. "I thought I was over it. Alex is still having nightmares, and I haven't been having any dreams about the fire, and I thought that must mean I'm okay." He bit at the corner of one nail and looked at her. "Clearly, I'm not."

She nods. "So how do we make you feel better?"

Nicholas pondered for a long time. He looked around the room and he looked at Jade and he thought about what might help. Eventually, his eyes flicked up, but with a slightly-forced half smile on his face, he said, "We could talk about the party."

"So, you *do* think I'm going to botch it!" she accused, cackling.

"I don't!" he swore. "I know you'll do good. You just...you know how I am about these things." He was confident in his friend's abilities but when it came to events, he hated surprises. He didn't enjoy being blindsided, because in not knowing he risked being unhappy and trying to show his thanks anyway. He felt anxiety over parties for the same reason he micromanaged his own wedding: he liked knowing how situations would go, liked preparing for them. Jade was trying to be nice and throw a party, but there was a place in the back of his mind where he wondered if she was going to do it the way he pictured, and that ate at him.

"At some point, Nicholas, you have to let someone else do something for you without panicking that everything will be all wrong," she said. "I'm not trying to add stress to your life by planning a party for you and Alex. I'm trying to take the stress away from you guys and let you have a party where you don't have to think about what you need to do for the event."

Nicholas knew this. Deep down, he knew it. She was clearly trying to show she cared. "Will you at least tell me what you are planning? Not for me to micromanage. Just for me to, I don't know, have a heads-up on things."

She laughed. "I can tell you one thing about it and ask you for your help on one thing, but that's your absolute limit, Mr. Control." She stood up and grabbed a notebook sitting on the counter. "You'll need to arrive at ten in the morning at Mandan Park a week from Saturday."

"That's seriously all you're going to tell me about it?" he asked, head tilted to one side.

"Yes. It is." She smirked. "Oh! And dress comfortable but not too formal. Springy, but not shabby. And definitely *not* overly fancy. I have a knee-length dress, and Veronica is going to wear cargo shorts and a blouse, if that gives you an idea of the dress code." That gave Nicholas no indication of the level of dress because a knee-length dress and cargo shorts implied two very different events. Still, he nodded. "Also, I need your recipe for those blueberry yogurt bars you made for V's Ostara breakfast last year."

Nicholas stood up and walked closer, coming to stand near her in the kitchen. "Sure. I can text that to you. Now, what's in the notebook?" His mischievous grin should have been enough to show her he was no threat. Now, though, snagging her notebook was all about his sense of pride. That, and he *really* wanted to know what her plan was.

"Nothing," she said, holding it behind her back tightly.

He poked her in the ribs. "Nothing, huh? Nothing at all?" His eyebrow quirked in distrust, but he kept smiling. A sense of normalcy returned, a glimmer of his life before, and for a moment his mind wasn't focused on the fire or the way everything had changed. This was how they always had been, Jade and him, goofing off and taunting each other. She lifted the notebook and held it up, trying to keep it out of his reach.

"You know that works better when I'm not a foot taller than you," he teased, reaching for it.

Veronica walked in and Jade whipped around and threw it to her. "V! Catch!"

Veronica did, shaking her head with mock disapproval. "Why do you two always put me in the middle of this? Hi, Nicholas." She gripped the notebook in her teeth as she slipped her shoes off and removed her scarf. When she pulled it out of her mouth, Jade tutted with disgust. "So, I take it Nicholas wants all the details about his party?"

"Guilty," Nicholas said. He turned to Jade and smiled. "I trust you. Okay? All jokes aside, I trust you." He wrapped his arms around her and hugged her close. "Thank you for doing this for us."

"You're welcome," Jade said. "And I know. I'd be more worried about you if you didn't try to butt your nose into the party planning process. I'd be over there checking your temperature and driving you to the hospital if you weren't here trying to steal my damn notebook."

Nicholas was happy to hear that. For every moment he feared he was being too intrusive, or Alex reminded him to relax over the party and let Jade do her thing, knowing that in the end, Jade didn't truly mind, helped a lot. "Okay. I'll see you a week from Saturday," he said, giving her another hug.

"You sure as hell better be seeing me before that," Jade said. "Or are you only in this friendship for the party?"

Nicholas laughed. "Come for dinner Tuesday?" he asked.

"Wouldn't miss it," Veronica answered for them both. "What are you making?"

"Whatever you want," Nicholas answered.

"Make that sticky biscuit stuff you made that one time and I'm in," Jade said. "Now, not to rush you out, but I've got a party to plan." She guided him to the door.

"Gee, I won't let the door hit me on the way out," Nicholas said, heading out of the door with a wave. This time, in the hall, he felt better. He no longer had the sting in his gut as he looked toward the other side of the hall, the turn leading to his apartment. His *old* apartment, he reminded himself.

Heading for the stairs, he froze. "Alex?"

"Hey, baby. What are you doing here?"

"I was just seeing Jade."

"Oh." Alex nodded slowly, biting his lip. "Cool. Checking up on the party?"

Nicholas smiled. "Yeah." It hit him then that Alex hadn't offered up what he was doing here, at their old place on this side of the building. "What are you doing here?"

"The insurance guy needed some extra photos. I just thought I'd snap some." Alex shifted his stance and for some reason, Nicholas had trouble believing him. "I'll be home in a bit?"

"Sure. I'll see you there." Nicholas hugged him and gave him a peck on the cheek. "Dinner will be ready quick tonight. Don't be too long?"

"Okay," Alex promised.

As Nicholas walked away, heading down the stairs and toward his car, uneasiness overwhelmed him once again. This time, it had nothing to do with the apartment and everything to do with the fact that he was completely, absolutely certain that Alex was lying to his face, and why? Nicholas hadn't the slightest idea. Alex never lied to him—or not that he knew of. And Alex was a terrible liar anyway. His body language was always a dead giveaway. The way he shifted or looked away... Nicholas knew his tells. He wondered for a moment if Alex was there to pry about the party too; maybe he was trying to get information so Nicholas wouldn't worry. That was the kind of thing Alex was good about—reassuring Nicholas.

Chapter Twelve

The Hardest Goodbye

Alex had never lied to Nicholas before. Sure, he'd lied in front of Nicholas, little things like excuses as to why they couldn't go out with friends, or why they'd shown up late to an event (usually so no one would know Nicholas had taken too long getting ready. Again). As a result, jitters shook through him as he walked toward Jade's apartment. What if Nicholas turned around and came looking for him in their old home? Alex had promised to be there. If Nicholas did turn around, that's where he'd expect to find him. So, Alex bypassed Jade's door altogether, making a beeline for the apartment he and Nicholas had shared days before. Taking a few more photos wouldn't hurt, even if he was sure he'd canvassed the whole place.

ALEX: *Nicholas caught me in the hallway*

ALEX: *I think I'm going to check the old apartment and then go home*

ALEX: *Sorry for keeping that stuff there longer*

JADE: *Don't worry about it. I would have texted and warned you, but he was pretty upset when he got here.*

ALEX: *About what?*

JADE: *Same thing we've all been upset about ever since the fire. Weird not having you guys here.*

ALEX: *I know. We miss you.*

ALEX: *I'll stop by tomorrow?*

JADE: *Sounds like a plan.*

He wasn't trying to lie to Nicholas, and he sure as heck wasn't trying to hurt him, but knowing he was doing exactly that made Alex miserable. His only goal was to rebuild what he'd broken. *That's not really deceit, right?* He kept telling himself that. Never mind the ache in his chest knowing this wasn't going to be home anymore. That hurt worse than anything.

As Alex photographed the apartment they'd called home again, standing in the living room, he started to feel sick. He studied the charred remains of the carpet and flooring in the room, looking down at the fibers beneath his feet. Standing near where they'd kissed for the first time, on the floor of the room where they'd shared intimacy for the first time, both in *that* sense and in the sense of watching movies and curling up, Alex's heart ached. He scanned the walls, finding a bare spot the fire hadn't touched not far from the couch. The bare spot stood in stark contrast to the charring of the framed pictures only inches away. In the empty space, he found a thumbtack. He walked over to reach up and pull it out, and he tucked it in his pocket. Their blanket forts. The one they'd had for the first time, and all the ones they'd snuggled in since. His heart broke. He hadn't let himself dwell on the stuff they'd lost of their shared history. He'd locked that away from reach. Now, there was nothing to keep him from realizing it. He looked at the wrecked television, broken on its stand, their movies beneath ruined. They'd already inventoried all the DVDs and sent the list to the rental insurance company, but insurance could only replace tangible objects. It couldn't bring back the memories, or the way their *Die Hard* case was slightly crushed, the way *Love Actually*'s plastic had been torn in a tickle fight. Insurance couldn't bring back the aspects that made their memories special. He was already sure the money wouldn't cover the items themselves in the first place.

Alex realized moving to a new apartment post-fire wasn't like moving from one place to another at all. In a planned move, one got to say goodbye to their home and belongings, take a moment to treasure the memories they had there, and then leave. But he and Nicholas hadn't gotten that. He pulled his phone out and called Nicholas.

"Hello?" Nicholas asked. "Everything going okay?"

"No, um." Alex's voice cracked as a tear streaked down his cheek. "Are you already at the apartment? Or are you still close by?"

"I'm about halfway there. Why?"

"Can you come back?" It hit him that they weren't calling the new apartment home yet. Neither of them was, really. His tears started to get more insistent. "I need us to do something."

"Okay. For the insurance, or...?"

"No," Alex said. "Just, um... Just come here. Please, baby." He squatted, trying to keep himself from toppling over. The room spun around him; his head a dizzy mess from the reality of what had happened.

"I'm on my way, okay? Stay there."

Nicholas was back to the remains of their home in minutes. As soon as Alex heard footsteps, he stood to greet him. "Hey." He wiped the tears with the back of his hand and tried not to make it so obvious he was crying.

"Oh, sweetheart..." Nicholas strode over and wrapped his arms around Nicholas. "What's wrong?"

"I was just thinking that we never got to really tell this place goodbye. The last time we were here we were so damn focused on the stuff," Alex said. "We never said goodbye. We never thanked our home for what it meant to us." He started to cry harder. He knew this was irrational. Of the two of them, Nicholas was the sentimental, sappy one. His own refusal to admit how hard this had hit him was painful and strange, and Nicholas held him and rocked him.

"You're right. We didn't. Let's do it now." Nicholas took his hand, and Alex walked him toward the kitchen, where it had all started.

Nicholas ran his hand over the table, fingertips coming back sooty. "This is where I was sitting when you came to yell at me for being too loud. The second time we ever met."

Alex laughed. "I was so annoyed. And so tipsy." He looked at the table. "We planned so much here. You made my proposal cookie here, and...and we worked on our wedding and our school and job applications and sorted recipes and played cards and had Jade and Veronica over for board games and that blueberry coffee cake you were hooked on for like a month and a half."

"It's a good coffee cake, to be fair." Nicholas smiled, reminiscing, and then took Alex's hand and led him to the living room.

"Here's where we had the blanket fort," Alex said before Nicholas could say anything. He reached in his pocket and pulled out the thumbtack. "I found this in the wall." He gestured toward where he'd discovered it.

"We did have the blanket fort, but I was thinking about the time I accidentally broke your nose." Nicholas bit his lip.

"Oh! Oh my gosh!" Alex rubbed at his nose and started to laugh. "I forgot all about that. I've never laughed so hard during intense pain in my life." They had been playing Extreme Spoons with Jade and Veronica, leaving the spoons across the apartment instead of in the center of the table, and Alex and Nicholas had both gotten four of a kind at once. They'd launched themselves over the couch and ran for the same spoon, colliding in the process as Alex tripped over Nicholas and smacked into the TV stand. Blood had gotten everywhere, but Alex had been victorious, winning the game. "I still won."

"You won because I felt bad for breaking you and let you win," Nicholas said, laughing as he walked to the TV stand. "Look."

A strip of unburnt carpet had a stain on it from the resulting nosebleed. "Well, we certainly left our mark on this place. Definitely wouldn't have gotten the deposit back."

"We did. And I think we'll leave our mark on the new one too." He led Alex to the window.

"This is the first place I ever really felt safe," Alex confessed to Nicholas, standing in front of the window.

"What do you mean?"

"I mean, everywhere I lived before was a struggle, like the house my parents had when they got divorced. When I think about that house, I think about the fights and the anger and the tension all the time. And then my grandparents' house when I'd live there in the summer. They don't accept me. It wasn't a home that made me feel like I could be me. And then in LA, there was my mom's depression, the fact that we squeezed into a small home just to scrape by, and I still hid so much of myself there. This is the first home I really blossomed in. The first place I was really *Alex.*" Alex had thought about that before, but he'd never said as much to Nicholas, never made it clear this was the first home he'd found true acceptance in, both from his peers and within himself. Losing it to a fire was so cosmically unfair.

"Alex..." Nicholas stepped forward and hugged him, holding him tightly, and Alex leaned his head on his shoulder, facing the window. He breathed in, focused more on Nicholas's scent than the sooty, smoky smell of the air around them. They were pressed so close together he could feel Nicholas speak as much as he could hear him. "You deserve safety. I hope that doesn't change now that we don't live here."

As Alex looked out of the window, he knew safety was found as much in the people he surrounded himself with as in a physical location, that moving wouldn't change anything. Letting go was hard. He could almost imagine the views they had out of the window in the past year. He pictured the twinkling lights the apartments behind theirs had put out. He imagined the flowers blooming in the bushes between the lower patios, and the succulents they'd planted when they'd failed to get flowers to bloom on their own balcony. He imagined the sound of the nearby pool, the laughter of people splashing and shouting in the summertime. The fall leaves were his favorite memory. When Nicholas had disappeared for a while outside and then called him to come look out of the window. Alex had, only to see Nicholas had raked them into a massive pile. "Come jump with me," he'd said. They'd spent the rest of the afternoon jumping in the leaves like children.

"Remember the snowman?" Nicholas asked.

"Which one?" After he'd made an ass of himself to Nicholas, he'd tried to apologize by building a snowman directly in sight of Nicholas's window, because from this angle, Nicholas couldn't see the army of snowmen he'd helped create. He'd never gone to so much effort to apologize to someone before, and that alone should have shown him how much Nicholas would mean to him. How much he already did, Alex thought.

"The second one."

That one, Alex had used to propose, a simple snowman with "Will you Marry Me?" on a sign around his neck. "I remember," he answered. He couldn't forget that. He lifted his phone and snapped a picture of the view from the window. It wouldn't do any good for the insurance, but the image would do a lot of good for his heart.

The bedroom had been almost untouched by the fire—the firefighters credited Nicholas having closed the door for how it had spared their belongings there—so they barely bothered to peek in and give it a quick goodbye. Most of their tangible memories had existed in the spaces where they lived rather than where they slept. Alex had said goodbye to the places that mattered. As Alex walked toward the door, hand in Nicholas's, he turned to him. "You ready?" he asked.

"Yeah," Nicholas said. He kissed his fingertips and pressed them to the door of their apartment. Then he cupped Alex's chin and kissed him. "Thanks, apartment, for the memories."

Alex muttered a "thank you," and then swiped at his tears. "I guess this is goodbye, isn't it?"

Nicholas nodded. "Yeah. I think it is."

Chapter Thirteen

Best Friends Forever

"Babe, I'm sure she did an amazing job," Alex said, holding Nicholas's hand and turning the radio down.

Nicholas snorted. He felt more than a little called out. "Is it that obvious?"

"That you're freaking out about whether or not this will turn out how you want it to?"

"Yeah."

"In that case? Yes. It's completely obvious." Alex drew Nicholas's hand to his lips and kissed his knuckles.

Alex was right; he was nervous as heck. There were so many different aspects to party planning, so many moving parts to coordinate, and even with Jade's promises it would be an amazing party, and with his confidence that she wanted to make the celebration perfect for him, he had his small doubts. That wasn't anything against Jade, and everything against Nicholas. He itched to micromanage every detail, the finer points of the party. He knew his obsessive need to control a situation was a horrible habit, and his tendency to over-plan and over-direct his friends when it came to party planning wasn't entirely helpful. Not when they wanted to do nice things for him.

Still, he didn't love the idea of going to a party and not playing a role in the planning. It was in his nature. Perhaps that was part of why he and Alex couldn't see eye to eye on weddings. Or maybe not weddings, but the scale of the celebrations. Nicholas couldn't be certain.

"Start with what you know," Alex said. "The party's at the park, right? The forecast says it'll be sunny and unseasonably warm all day. That's *good*."

"She needed a recipe from me. My blueberry yogurt bars," Nicholas said. "Given the dish and the time, I'm assuming it's a brunch-type event." He pulled his car into the parking lot.

"You love brunch. And you love parks. And more than anything else, you love Jade. Take a deep breath, and let's do this."

Nicholas did, putting the car into park as he inhaled and exhaled slowly.

"Another."

Nicholas did that too. Inhaling. Exhaling. "Good?" He took two more deep breaths for good measure.

"Good."

Nicholas didn't mean to come off as ungrateful. He *was* incredibly grateful. He loved what Jade had done for him and the effort she'd put in. He was just uncomfortable about letting go of that control. "Okay. I'm ready." He opened his car door, walked around to Alex's side, and opened his door also. As they walked to shelter three, he held Alex's hand and Alex thumbed over his knuckles to keep him calm. He had a gift for Jade in his other hand, a small gesture of his appreciation. Nothing much—a gourmet cheese ball from a shop she and Veronica especially liked and some crackers to go with it—but he knew they'd love it.

As they made their way over the hill and down to the shelter, any amount of nervousness he had faded away. Jade knew him so well. There was color coordination! Tablecloths! Balloons! Jade couldn't have created a more Nicholas-style event. Everything was perfect. He dropped Alex's hand and raced toward Jade. "Oh my gosh, it's beautiful," he told her as he hugged her tightly.

"Do you trust me now?"

"Always," Nicholas said. But she poked him in the ribs in response, and he admitted, "Usually."

Alex caught up, smiling and giving her a tight hug. "Thank you for doing this." As Alex released her, he turned and gasped. "Whoa, this is amazing."

"It really is," Nicholas agreed. The party was even more stunning up close.

"This *had* to be amazing. You guys deserve something good." Her hands stayed on the small of their backs as she guided them to the bar cart. "First, though, cocktails." The other guests were trickling in.

Jade had taken the gorgeous colors of the shower curtain and lightened them for springy pastels, the coral and blue dominant, with mint and gold accents. Alex's fingers grazed a gold balloon reading "Mr. and Mr." If Nicholas had planned the party himself, he would have selected tablecloths in different pastel colors, each matching the color scheme perfectly. And Jade knew him well enough she'd done exactly that, allowing the party to coordinate in the most delightful way. The side of the shelter had a table set up with brunch foods, all kept hot in Crock-Pots and warming trays, alongside platters of fresh fruit. She truly had taken everything they liked into consideration, and Nicholas couldn't be more grateful.

Even Jade looked amazing, wearing a knee-length dress matching the pastel-coral color of the party, with black accents. She'd really outdone herself. "Here," Nicholas said, handing her the bag. "We brought you a little gift. Thank you for this." No matter how many thanks he and Alex gave, it wouldn't be enough.

As the rest of the guests arrived, Nicholas looked around at all their closest friends. Jade had invited everyone they loved, or at least, everyone who lived close enough to come, and the idea that she had put so much effort into making them smile brought tears to his eyes. He was no longer nervous, but instead, he realized he hadn't needed to be in the first place.

"Come on, guests of honor. Your drinks," she said, presenting them with the promised drinks. Jade picked up a glass, stuffed with cotton candy, and poured a sweet vanilla vodka over it before topping it with clear soda. Per Jade's usual standard, the cocktails were extra strong. Nicholas saw Alex wince at his first sip, and he grabbed the soda to top him off with a less intense drink as Jade greeted Brandon and his girlfriend, Olivia.

"Thanks," Alex said, giggling. "I don't think she'd ever make it as a bartender, but she is one hell of a best friend."

"Yeah, she is," Nicholas said, hand on Alex's back as he guided him toward their friends.

Mostly, the party was all about hugs. Throughout the beginning of the brunch, Alex and Nicholas hugged every person at least a few times, both through condolences about the fire and through congratulations on their engagement months before. Of course, everyone in attendance had already congratulated them, but now the joy was kicking into overdrive, a party celebrating the next stage of their life together.

Nicholas walked along the buffet table. In line with Jade's request for his recipe, Nicholas's blueberry yogurt bars were the sweet star of the show, but Veronica's Texas-style potatoes were the true savory hit of the party, the dishes a perfect contrast to one another. As Nicholas filled his plate, Brandon walked up behind him. They'd been friends for most of Nicholas's post-grad career, and only now did Nicholas realize he'd barely talked to him since the fire.

"Hey!" Brandon said, grabbing a lemon cake pop and putting it on his plate.

"Hey," Nicholas answered.

"How are you holding up?" That was the hardest question, since it implied they *looked* like they weren't over the fire yet. Of course, they weren't. No one was pressuring them to move on from what they'd lost, but something about the words, the concern in their voices, tinged the party with a sense of sadness instead of the joy it deserved.

But Nicholas didn't want to say that or make waves at the party, a happy celebration of his love. Instead, he smiled at Brandon and said, "We're adjusting. Right now, we're focusing on the good. We're alive, we're in love, and our apartment has a bathtub, so we're taking full advantage of the positive side of the situation."

Brandon laughed. "A bathtub? Man, I'm coming over. I haven't had an actual bath in two years. Showers don't hit the same way." There was truth in the statement, but it had also diverted Brandon away from the need for them to mourn what once was.

"You're welcome anytime. We miss being on that side of town." He knew they were long overdue for inviting everyone over to their place, and Brandon's girlfriend had stopped by to deliver meals, like Veronica and Jade had, but they hadn't done any sort of full-fledged dinner party at their new home. They were still—like Nicholas said—adjusting. Having guests hadn't felt right yet.

Alex walked up and gave Brandon a side-hug. "Pass me a cake pop?"

Brandon smiled and grabbed one for Alex, looking back and forth between them. "I don't think I've ever seen any couple more well suited to each other than the two of you."

Nicholas wasn't sure the statement was entirely true. Jade and Veronica were a perfect match, and Nicholas could see the love in their eyes from across the park shelter as Veronica laughed at whatever Jade was saying. The fact that the two of them could crack each other up every single time was inspiring to Nicholas. He wanted to model his relationship after theirs in so many ways: mutual trust and respect, undying love, and a sense of running head-first toward each other's goals. He turned back to Brandon, watching as Olivia came up closer to him and kissed his cheek.

"I think we're all very, very lucky," he told Brandon, smiling at him sincerely. He scanned the party. The people they loved were happy. They were happy. A sense of *home* filled his chest.

*

Alex settled in next to Veronica, reaching a hand over to squeeze hers as he said, "Hey, this seat taken?"

She shook her head. "All yours, sweetie."

Somehow, by way of Nicholas and Jade's friendship, they'd formed a friendship too. Veronica was a lot more similar to him than Jade was, and as much as he adored Jade, he was endlessly happy to see an open seat beside Veronica. He loved the laid-back sentiment of the party. For as much as Jade had worked to make the party suit Nicholas nicely, she'd made it suit him, too, without a central table for him and Nicholas to sit at and be the center of attention, and without all the fanfare. She'd assured him there would be toasts later, so Nicholas wasn't missing any of the essentials, and...some kind of craft time? He wasn't sure what to make of that. But he was happy to have a spare moment with Veronica, just a second to talk and not hug anyone else for a few minutes until he got his bearings again.

"Thanks for the potatoes. They're amazing." In all honesty, he couldn't convey enough thanks. The potatoes, the party, the...everything.

"Oh, they're not all that," Veronica said, waving him off. "The French toast is where it's at." She nudged him with her shoulder. "So. I was thinking. Usually, engagement parties are for little gifts, y'know, picture frames and vases and stuff. But you guys need a lot more than that after the fire, don't you?"

Alex shrugged. They'd picked up a lot of stuff but admitting they still had major gaps in their apartment was hard. Even what they had was mostly secondhand, garage sale finds. All usable, certainly, but not necessarily what he and Nicholas would have picked. "Every time I think we've got it all sorted out, that we have everything replaced and back to normal, we go to do something and realize what we're missing. The other day Nicholas went to bake a cake and I realized all our glass baking stuff had shattered in the fire. I had to update our registry, and then we didn't get to have cake. I guess we could have gone and bought what we needed, but who wants to make that kind of effort for cake?"

"Damn," Veronica said. "And if you lived in the building, you guys could have borrowed ours, but it's not really feasible to drive to borrow a baking dish."

"Not at seven in the morning, no," Alex answered.

"Plus, we would have required a cake tax. You use our pan, Nicholas bakes us cake." She winked at him and took a bite of her French toast. "What kind of cake was it?"

"That sticky biscuit one he makes all the time."

"Ooh, yeah. Definitely a cake tax," she said, laughing.

Talking about the fire was getting easier for Alex. He felt he could tell her honestly how everything was okay, but it also wasn't okay. A sense of unease came with how much they were having to change their lives around because of the fire. He'd submitted some assignments late, too, having lost them when his laptop went up in flames. Life was just...different now. He studied the group of people there, all gathered to give Alex and Nicholas their love and support, and he realized every single one of them had the fire in the back of their minds. He looked at Veronica and said, "I still feel guilty."

"Oh, honey," Veronica told him, wrapping an arm around his shoulders and rubbing his bicep. "This wasn't your fault. Things happen, and you didn't start the fire."

Alex nodded. "I guess I figured by this point, I'd be able to focus on other stuff, but I can't fully get engrossed in anything without the fire nagging at me." At only two weeks out from the fire, his reaction was probably normal, but normal or not, he hated that he couldn't enjoy life when that lingered in his mind.

"It's going to stay like that for a little while, Alex. Eventually, you two will find the new normal. One day you won't find something you're missing every time you go to bake or watch a movie or have guests over. You'll stop stubbing your toe as you learn how the furniture is arranged, and you'll realize you've made it. You probably won't even notice until one day you'll think about the fire and you'll realize you haven't done that in a while," Veronica explained.

"Oh," Alex nodded. He narrowed his eyes. "Wait, how do you know that's how it'll happen?"

"Because I've been there. My whole house went up in flames when I was twelve. We lost everything. I lost my favorite childhood stuffed animal. And for months, Gooby the Bear was all I could think about. Every friend at school would only want to hear about the fire. Some rumors flew around that my family *set* the fire because we were poor and needed an insurance payout. And every day we had those moments where something would be missing. My sister's retainer case, a spare set of sheets for my little brother's bed, the type of brush my mom used on the days where her hair was extra out of control..." She sighed and looked up at him, pushing her plate away. "Eventually, stuff got replaced and we'd only be missing things sometimes, like when we would be decorating our new Christmas tree and go to look for an ornament that wasn't there, some handprint ornament one of us had made in school, and we realized it had been months since we'd thought about the fire or talked about it. And that's when we knew we were better, even if those moments still hurt."

Alex considered it carefully. "That makes sense." It didn't stop his worry that some issues would never go away, like the bad dreams he'd had about the heat or sound or smell, or the unease he felt, but saying goodbye to the apartment had helped. He hadn't been tempted to look at the place they'd lived, or at what they'd lost. "Thanks, V."

Nicholas sat down and joined him at the table, hand reaching for Alex's. "You two having a good chat?" he asked.

"Yeah. A very good one." Alex smiled and leaned his head on Nicholas's shoulder, and then gave his shoulder a quick peck before eating the potatoes on his plate.

*

"Put that trash bag down," Jade said, coming up behind Alex after the party. A flower crown rested on her head after their craft moment that turned out to be surprisingly fun. Her voice lifted with a slight laugh, a twinge of humor in it, and Alex smiled and kept putting paper plates in the trash. His own flower crown started to slip down his forehead.

"You can't make me. You're not my mom," Alex joked, turning to stick his tongue out at her.

"Oh, I'm not? Because last I checked, you come to me anytime you have a problem," she giggled. "I think I qualify. If not as your mom, as your life coach."

"Or, uh...maybe a spiritual advisor?" Alex rolled his eyes at her, smirked, and kept cleaning. "Thanks for the party, Jade."

"I swear if you two thank me one more time..." She put paper plates into Alex's bag. "You realize I did this because I love you? No thanks necessary. You're my best friends. Don't tell V, because she's supposed to be my best best friend." She elbowed him gently in the ribs.

"Your secret is safe with me." Alex smirked. "Speaking of V, how am I just now finding out she went through a fire as a kid?"

Jade shrugged. "She doesn't like to talk about it. That's where the scar on her arm is from. From the fire."

Alex looked down at his own arm, at the singed hair that was already growing back. "I didn't realize she'd been hurt. I barely notice the scar on her arm, honestly." Most of the time, Veronica wore long sleeves. Even in the summer, she'd wear tops with sheer sleeves covering her arms. He'd always thought it was a style choice. "I'm very thankful for her. And for you."

Jade smiled, hand patting Alex's. "I know. And we're thankful for you two. Now, we have a whole dozen extra cake pops, so don't forget to take them with you."

Alex understood. Talking about the pain from what happened was hard, and today was about the good, about their friendship and love and future. "Hey, J?"

"Yeah?"

"I have an idea." He paused, turning to Nicholas and waving him over.

Nicholas gave a small hug to their old neighbor, Alice, and then walked toward him. "What's up?"

"I probably should have discussed this with Nicholas before asking you, but I was thinking, and I already know he'll be on board, so we may as well talk about this now." He turned to Nicholas and studied the puzzled, amused expression on his face.

"You're sure I'm on board?" Nicholas asked.

"Yes. Just...shush and listen." He turned his attention back to Jade. "Jade, I was thinking—"

"You were thinking? Yeah, I can see the smoke coming out of your ears," Jade joked.

"Oh my gosh! If you don't both chill for a second, I'm going to slap you both and tell you to forget it," Alex said, cracking up. Leave it to Jade and Nicholas to distract him from the task at hand. He turned toward Nicholas. "We haven't picked an officiant for our wedding yet, have we?"

"No."

Alex turned back to Jade. "Jade, what if you married us? Like, what if you officiate our wedding?"

She cocked her head to one side, looking back and forth between them.

Nicholas beamed. "Please?" he asked, wrapping an arm around Alex's waist. Alex knew him well enough to know he'd agree without any sort of previous consultation. "I don't know why I didn't think to ask you to do that sooner. I guess I wasn't thinking, actually. You'd be the perfect person."

Tears welled in Jade's eyes, and she brought both hands to cover her mouth from the sob Alex could already hear in her voice. She nodded and stepped forward, and Alex, completely from instinct, wrapped his arms around her. Nicholas did the same. "Yes!" she managed between them. "Obviously, yes."

Alex kissed her hair and gave her a squeeze. Regardless of what happened, or anything that had led up to it, their wedding was going to be beautiful. Alex had no doubt in his mind.

Chapter Fourteen

Breakfast in Bed

Nicholas had brought Alex breakfast in bed almost every Saturday morning for a year and four months, with few exceptions. They'd tapered off a little during Alex's illness, and missed a couple of weekends after the fire. And a few times, they'd skipped it to meet Jade and Veronica for brunch, but most Saturdays that moment of connection was a staple of their weekend routine.

Alex wasn't complaining. He enjoyed the breakfasts, the time spent together, and the way it eased them into the weekend. Sometimes he did it on other occasions too; other times he got up and made the effort because a chilly Tuesday in October warranted a celebration and Nicholas said he wanted to bring Alex waffles or bacon and eggs for no reason at all. Whenever Alex mentioned it, people seemed thrown off guard. Brandon had first assumed their little tradition was a birthday thing, and Jade agreed there was no way anyone—even Nicholas—would be working that hard to woo their partner a year and four months into the relationship. But it wasn't Nicholas's style to stop a good tradition.

Food was Nicholas's love language. Or one of them. Taking care of the people he loved, that was the real language he spoke.

And Alex loved waking up to the smell of bacon and the sound of sausage sizzling in a pan, or the taste of his favorite iced coffee to wash pastries down. Nicholas knew his favorites, knew every breakfast food he liked best. And Alex showed his appreciation any way he could.

But as the move and the fire changed how often Nicholas could bring him breakfast in bed, Alex adjusted. He missed their routine, but he knew life was hectic lately. They were still getting back in the swing of things, and Nicholas treated him with morning meals of homemade toaster pastries, or a freezer full of bacon and sausage burritos for anytime they didn't wake up early enough for a full spread, or weekdays when Alex would be headed out of the door quickly to get to work before his midday classes.

Today was not a breakfast in bed morning. Alex blinked, his eyes opening in slivers to block out the bright sunlight as much as possible. They'd forgotten to close the blinds again and hadn't yet replaced the blackout curtains that helped them sleep in late on weekend mornings like they had at their old apartment. The old ones weren't damaged by the fire much, but they smelled like smoke and dampness and there was no way they wanted to bring that into their new apartment. The sun pouring through the open blind slats stung. Groaning, Alex threw an arm across his eyes as he rolled over. "It's so freaking bright," he whined. Sunlit mornings might have been a source of optimism for most about the great day ahead, but an excessively light morning was never Alex's idea of a good time. Not on the one day of the week he could sleep in, the one where he didn't have to be up before the sun to make coffee for undercaffeinated students.

"What time is it?" Nicholas mumbled beside him, pulling the blanket up and over both of their shoulders.

"Seven twelve." When they'd first met, Alex would have assumed Nicholas was a morning person. The early morning snowman building events, his optimistic personality, all of it added up to make Alex think Nicholas would always be up before the sun. That wasn't the case though. Not without protest, and definitely not easily. Sure, Nicholas saw the good in every moment of the day, and he was more of a morning person than Alex. Nicholas could appreciate a morning at least a little bit, whereas Alex thought he was being dragged through hell every time he had to wake up before ten, which was almost every day of the week. But Nicholas wasn't a morning person in the sense of what that usually meant. No, Nicholas was a morning person as a byproduct of being an all-the-time person, the kind of person who took delight in all hours of the day.

Right now, Nicholas seemed to be finding joy in soft blankets, and Alex decided to snuggle closer for warmth. That was another thing Alex appreciated on early mornings. Nicholas was a naturally warm person. Not just in his personality but in his body temperature as well. For every night Alex had cold toes, Nicholas's feet were warm, and he rubbed them gently against Alex's. For every time he shivered because the fan was blowing too harshly, there was a time when Nicholas would curl between him and the cool air, soaking it in for himself as he acted as a barrier for Alex. This morning was no exception. Nicholas was a space heater.

"Morning," Nicholas mumbled against Alex's shoulder, wrapping an arm around his waist tightly as he held him close.

"Morning."

"I forgot to make breakfast."

"You didn't forget," Alex said sleepily. "I woke up first." His answers were lagging and slow, his brain running on a delay from tiredness. "You don't have to make it. We have...uh...burritos." Words slurred from his mouth, drool present in the corner of his lips. His eyes shut again as he tried to soak in the last few minutes of sleep before he knew his brain would force him to fully wake up.

"Mm-hmm," Nicholas replied. As he trailed his hand down Alex's abs, Alex realized breakfast wasn't the main thing on Nicholas's mind. This was better than breakfast in bed. The feeling of Nicholas's hand working its way down his skin? *That* made a morning interesting. Alex rocked back against Nicholas, his hard length against the curve of Alex's ass. Yeah, this was a welcome substitute indeed.

"*Good* morning," Alex emphasized, rolling over in Nicholas's arms. He would have stayed like he was, letting Nicholas do what he'd initiated, but Alex wanted more, wanted to make it a good morning for them both. He kept his eyes mostly closed. As much as he wanted to see Nicholas's face, the bright morning light was too much for him. Instead, he allowed his hands and his intuition, his intimate knowledge of Nicholas's body, to guide the way for him, hooking his thumbs into the waistband of Nicholas's boxer briefs. He slid them down a little, to

Nicholas's knees, hands dragging along the skin so he could know how far he had gone.

"Are your eyes closed for any particular reason?" Nicholas laughed. "Or do I just look that bad in the mornings?"

"No, it's...sun's bright," Alex mumbled, chuckling and leaning in. He hoped Nicholas would take the hint and kiss him. Thankfully, he did. The kiss was soft and languid, something easy and gentle. They explored each other's lips and tongues. After this long, neither of them was particularly worried about morning breath. They were used to the smells and tastes, a unique sense of their bodies by now. There was no shame, no embarrassment about the bad breath, despite each of them teasing the other about it from time to time.

Sometimes, getting up to brush their teeth wasn't worth postponing alone time together. Today was one of those days.

Alex nuzzled at him, kissing Nicholas's jaw as Nicholas crept his hand down farther. "Morning," he repeated.

Alex grinned. "Keep going and I think you'll be giving me something better than breakfast." They had a running joke, not a slight toward what Nicholas did when he'd go out of his way to make him breakfast. Nicholas put in a lot of effort for him, cooking like that. Alex knew how much work it took, and Nicholas knew he appreciated that work. But for Alex, breakfast versus sex? A coin toss. Some days, eggs or bacon were exactly what he needed. Other days, this scratched an itch food couldn't.

As Nicholas's fingers wrapped around him, Alex gasped and his eyes fluttered open. "Yeah...that's...that's good, dang."

"Best kind of breakfast sausage?" Nicholas quipped, chuckling at his own joke as his hand worked Alex slowly, using a lot of care and the movements Alex liked best.

Alex's hand found Nicholas easily and he closed his eyes again. "Nah. Clearly *this* is the superior morning meat." He laughed. They shared so much of the same sense of humor, the same quips and inside jokes. Alex remembered a time he had once feared he'd never fit in with Nicholas's circle, not enough to get their shared humor and ease with one another. Now, the two of them had inside jokes even their circle of friends weren't privy to. "Good *morning!*" Alex moaned when Nicholas hit a particularly perfect spot, his thumb caressing a sensitive place just below the head.

Nicholas chuckled again. "Morning," he said.

Alex arched into the touch and rolled onto his back to get a better angle to touch Nicholas, and letting Nicholas get a better angle for him. In the mornings, hands worked perfectly, and neither of them made any effort to move it past that. Nicholas's hand moved faster, so Alex's hand moved faster. The two of them stroked in sync with each other, listening to breaths and feeling every movement. In this way, they knew their partner's needs. Intimately, they knew what the other needed and sensed what the other was asking for without a single word. When Nicholas leaned in to kiss Alex, Alex didn't have to have his eyes fully open to know the touch was coming; he kissed him back instinctively, exploring his mouth with his tongue. The vibration of the kisses when they experienced pleasure like this was one of the things Alex enjoyed most. They couldn't disconnect from each other long enough to make moans audible, the way they were whimpering and gasping. The sensations were needy in the best ways.

Alex arched his back and let his free hand move to Nicholas's beard and tug it. "I love you." There was a tenderness to their morning moments, a softness and sweetness that didn't extend to the rest of the day. Not that the rest of their time together wasn't soft and sweet, and not that intimacy wasn't as good in the afternoon or night, but it all carried a different weight under the haze of sleep and the light coming in through the windows.

"I love you too," Nicholas said, his hand still working. He hooked a leg over Alex's legs, moving until he was straddling him. As they grazed against each other in an attempt to find the pleasure they both sought, Nicholas wrapped a hand around them both. He took over for Alex, and Alex traced gentle lines on Nicholas's back with his fingers instead.

They communicated so clearly with so few words, a deep innate gentleness that largely went unspoken. A year before, two years before, he wouldn't have imagined sex could be like this, that intimacy could be so unspoken and yet so obvious, no miscommunication present. His lips found the place above Nicholas's collarbone, the hollow of skin dipping and curving around his muscles, some long held from his baking and others new growth from the prewedding workouts they'd been catching up on. He worked his mouth along his skin, first with peppered kisses and then with marks he sucked to the surface as Nicholas drew him closer to the edge. Later, Alex knew he'd admire the small purple-blue hickeys he'd made, but that was how Nicholas liked it anyway, small specks of love on top of his freckles. The marks made it clear Alex had, in many ways, claimed his heart. He'd told Alex as much time and time again.

Alex moaned against his skin, breath sucked out of him, oxygen pulled from his lungs as he stopped touching and instead grasped the sheets. "I'm so close," he said softly.

"Good," Nicholas said.

Nicholas captured his mouth in a kiss, hand stroking them together, slick against each other. In that moment, Alex felt safe and warm and comfortable, tugging Nicholas's lip between his teeth. He only released the kiss when he threw his head back to gasp air. "Oh gosh, yeah...right—" Right there, he'd tried to say, but his words were cut off with his shuddering cry, the shake in his body as he finished between them.

"I've got you, sweetheart," Nicholas said, but then he joined Alex, too, face buried in his neck as he stuttered out the sounds of his own release. Their breath was ragged, quick, and shattering the morning silence for a moment or two before Nicholas rolled off him.

"Morning," Alex repeated with a small giggle, dragging his fingers through their shared release.

"Morning," Nicholas answered. "So, what do you think? Should I go make breakfast and bring it to you, or...?"

"I thought this *was* my breakfast in bed." Alex laughed as he tugged Nicholas in for one more kiss. "Thank you. For offering, I mean. It's our day off. Let's go out to eat."

"Yeah?"

"Yeah. As soon as my legs will cooperate and not be complete jelly, we'll go shower." Alex smiled and looked up at the ceiling, thankful he had good ways and good reasons to wake up. Standing, he looked around at their new apartment, and realized that until he stood up and saw where he was, he hadn't thought about the fire when he first woke up the way he had been every day for weeks. Maybe Veronica was right.

Chapter Fifteen

Finished Product

Alex pasted business cards into the last page of the binder he'd been working for three weeks to create. "I think it's done, guys," he announced. Most of the binder, he'd put together at the coffee shop on his breaks. He'd contacted as many people as he could, as many businesses Nicholas might have met at various expos. Some of the binder, he'd done after work, under the guise of "a long shift," as he'd told Nicholas. But over the past week, the binder had gotten too bulky to transport properly. Instead, he'd taken to solely working on the project at Jade and Veronica's apartment.

"Finished?" Jade asked. "Can I see?"

"Sure." Alex opened the binder to the first page as she settled into the chair beside him. "Here it is." As she flipped through the pages, he spent more time studying her face than the work he'd completed. He wanted to see her true reaction, and besides, he'd already seen the binder several times.

"Nice," she said.

"That tone of voice says 'not nice.' What'd I mess up on?" If anyone knew what Nicholas wanted his wedding to be like, Jade did. She'd listened to him talk for hours on end after she'd eloped. And, aside from Alex and Nicholas, she had seen the old binder more than anyone else had.

"It is nice," she said. "If I say nice, I mean it's nice." Still, her face didn't match up with what she was saying.

Alex shook his head. "There's more that you want to say. Say it; it won't hurt my feelings."

"It's just..."

"Here we go," Veronica said from across the room, sipping a mug of tea. Usually when Jade started with an "it's just..." they were in for a trip. Usually, Alex would be laughing at how well he and Veronica both knew her, but now, her "it's just..." made his stomach sink. He promised he wouldn't be hurt, but those words made him worry he underestimated what she had to say.

"You made a great binder, Alex. I'm not sure it's the wedding Nicholas actually wants," Jade said.

"It's almost exactly what he'd planned before! I picked up the same magazines he'd been using and tried to find the same suits and yeah, some of the stuff he had was outdated or from magazines I can't *get* anymore, but this was the current plan as of the last time I saw the binder. It's *exactly* what Nicholas wants!" Alex protested. He didn't know the binder perfectly, but he knew the pages well enough, the aesthetics and the ideas. Anything they'd decided on, Alex had pasted in exactly as they'd decided it. Anything they hadn't, he'd pasted in the same types of options Nicholas had been picking between. "This is what he wants!" His phone buzzed with an email confirming their engagement photography session, the specific type of session he'd mapped out in the photography section of the binder, the detailed rain-themed photoshoot of his dreams. He tapped out a quick reply; he'd tell Nicholas about it later. Right now, his focus was on the binder and on Jade's reaction to it.

"Oh, I absolutely think it's what Nicholas *thinks* he wants," Jade said. "That doesn't mean it's the wedding he wants." She pursed her lips and kept flipping. "The binder itself is great. I wouldn't change a thing about it. Other than...none of it is *you*, and none of what you have here is what he really wants. You know him, Alex. You know how he can get so set on what he's planned that he loses sight of that being what he really wants to do."

"This is what he wants!" Alex insisted. "Big wedding. Flower arches and three camera angles and a butterfly release and all of our friends and a massive cake and a big candy bar that guests can visit and take their fill as favors. All of this, he wants for sure." Alex had listened to him talk about these details for hours, picking between this subtle shade of pink M&M or this custom teal gumdrop or the cream-colored Sixlets he had found online. The decisions were exhausting, but it all led to Alex being absolutely certain this was the right plan all along, that the binder, exactly how he'd made it, was precisely what Nicholas wanted. And he wanted to give that to him. Nicholas deserved his dream wedding, even if it wasn't Alex's dream.

"Alex, listen to me. You've done a great job with the binder. You have. But you know what Nicholas values most? Family. Friends. The people closest to him. He's going to talk up a big wedding, but this planner is missing the part of his wedding he needs the most."

Alex tugged at his hair, tears forming at his eyes. "I made it as much like his as I could." He knew she was right. Nicholas loved his family and friends over anything, the people in his life, and the wedding in the binder really didn't highlight that. Still, he'd worked so hard on it.

Veronica walked over and looked over his shoulder, hands resting on his shoulders as she gave them a squeeze. "J, the binder really does look like the old one," she said gently.

Jade nodded. "I know. I know that. That's why I said it's nice."

"But it's not *right*," Alex groaned. "Clearly." He pressed at his eyes with the heels of his hands, trying not to let his frustration get the best of him before snapping the binder shut. "I think I'm going to keep working on it. To try to get the wedding he wants...or whatever. I know I said today would be the last day, but I obviously need some more time. Can I leave it longer?" He was sweaty, a physical manifestation of his anxiety he couldn't currently scrub off his skin, and heat rose in his cheeks. Jade hadn't meant to embarrass him or hurt him, and he understood she was giving him the good kind of criticism he needed to make this binder the best possible gift, but the critique stung all the same. Alex wasn't the same sort of perfectionist Nicholas was, but he was a perfectionist all the same.

"Of course," Veronica said, squeezing his shoulders again. "Take all the time you need. Always."

Chapter Sixteen

Call it All Off

The ringing phone snapped Nicholas awake at eight on a Sunday morning. He swatted at the bedside table, grabbing for it, but Alex had already jumped up and gone around the table to pick it up. "Hello?"

Nicholas peeked his eyes open and watched Alex talk.

"Oh no. Are you seri—yeah, no, I'm so sorry. I'm...of course. We'll pay for the session, of course. I'm so sorry," Alex said apologetically. Nicholas sat bolt upright and looked at him, eyes wide. "No, we, uh. We had a house fire, and it slipped our mind...yes, we use a digital calendar, but I must have gotten it mixed up with everything going o—I know. I'm sorry." The look on Alex's face was absolutely grief-stricken. Nicholas hadn't seen a look quite like that in a while. He cocked his head to one side. "Yes, thank you. I really appreciate you offering to do that. Let me talk to my fiancé and then I'll get back with you. Thank you. Seriously." He nodded a few times and if Nicholas hadn't been aware of the concern on his face, he might have chuckled at the fact that the person on the other end of the phone couldn't see him nod. "You have a good day too. I'm sorry. Again. Okay...thank you. Bye."

"What was that?" Nicholas asked. Alex sank onto the bed beside him and buried his head in his hands. "Alex?"

"I messed up." His voice was muffled against his hands, and he still didn't look up.

"Messed what u—oh no. The photos," Nicholas said. Alex glanced up and nodded sadly. A pit formed in Nicholas's stomach. His perfect engagement photos, and they'd missed their shoot. "They didn't send a confirmation email on the date? No reminders?"

Alex went pale. "I'm so sorry."

"So, they did confirm. And..."

"And I was in the middle of something, and I pushed it away and forgot to... I forgot."

"You forgot our engagement photos. The one thing that I had said was most important right now, the one I was banking on after we'd lost everything else we'd planned. After...after everything, at least we had this photo session. And you...forgot." Nicholas clenched his teeth. His heart was racing. How many more ways could their wedding go wrong? Of *course,* the photos would be screwed up too. Nicholas was past frustrated. He choked a laugh. Now, the mishaps were almost comical, or they would be, if they didn't make his chest hurt.

"Nicholas, I made a mistake. They said that they'll move our deposit to another date if we rebook, so it isn't all lost," Alex insisted.

"Yeah, I mean... I can see how the slip-up happened. I think it's just, when something isn't your priority, it's easy to forget about it." Nicholas knew he was being unreasonable. Alex hadn't missed the photo session intentionally, but after all the other setbacks, he didn't know how not to be upset. His tone wasn't even snarky. Instead, he sounded defeated. He was giving up. Alex had shown him so many ways that this wasn't what he wanted, and Nicholas had kept pushing for it. Maybe now he needed to give in and stop fighting Alex about the wedding. "I don't know how many more ways you can show this isn't the wedding you want."

"What do you mean?" Alex asked.

"The binder, the photographer, asking to elope again and again and again... Just say it, Alex." Nicholas knew he was going down the wrong road. He could picture himself driving toward the invisible cliff, and when he should have been putting his foot on the brake, he kept pumping the gas on the argument instead. He couldn't stop himself.

"Say *what?*" Alex pleaded, standing up to face Nicholas. The tears in his eyes stung because Nicholas knew this argument hurt him too.

"Say you don't want our wedding to happen. If you did, this wouldn't keep happening. You wouldn't keep sabotaging things again and again!" Nicholas's hurt and frustration morphed to anger in an instant. That's what it ultimately had been: a series of mistakes leading to subconscious sabotage. Accidents could only be accidents so many times over.

Alex's face turned beet red at the accusation, crimson with anger. "So that's what you think this is? Sabotage? That I'm sitting here thinking, 'hmm, how can I screw up our wedding today?' Yeah, okay. That makes a lot of sense. I've worked my butt off day after day to—you know what? Yeah, actually. I'm frustrated. I'm annoyed you never listen to what I say about the wedding. Everything out of your mouth is 'big wedding this' and 'big wedding that.' Have you ever stopped and looked at the fact that you're planning the wedding sixteen-year-old you wanted, and I'm sitting here staring at my future husband, twenty-five years old, thinking *really*? This isn't what you want now. I know you better than that. I also know you're too stubborn to admit it!"

"What do you want from me?" Nicholas tensed, turning away from Alex.

"You know what I want? You really want to know? I want to be with you. I want to spend our lives together. You know what *you* want? A circus." Alex stomped to the bathroom and closed the door, and Nicholas heard the lock right after.

He sank onto the bed and started to sob, a choked gurgling in his throat as the tears started to flow. All he'd wanted was to marry Alex, and for it to be a beautiful wedding. A once-in-a-lifetime event because ultimately, that's what it was. The inevitable, the forever, the display of the start of their lifetime of love.

And Alex admitting he didn't want it that way, whether Nicholas had already known or not, was a blow. If all Alex wanted to do was elope, then what was the point of getting married in the first place? "Oh." Nicholas spoke to himself and the empty room around him. "What's the point in the first place?"

His heart sank. He stood up and knocked on the door. Nothing.

"Alex?" he asked, knocking again. No answer. "Alex!" he urged.

"What? You going to accuse me of starting World War I next?" Alex asked. Nicholas could hear the strain from tears in his voice.

"No. Don't be ridiculous, Alex." Silence. "I'm sorry. That was the wrong thing to say. Can you come out here? Please?"

"Sure." Nicholas heard the lock turn just before the door swung open. "What?"

Nicholas stood there and inhaled, then exhaled. "The wedding I want isn't the wedding you want, right?"

"Right."

"But you want to be with me, right?" Nicholas asked, voice shaking.

"Of course!" Alex said, brows furrowed. "You think that because I disagree with you on the wedding, I want to throw the whole...whole relationship away? Why, is that what you want? Your big wedding or we break up?"

"No!" He'd definitely asked the wrong question there, and he knew it. "No. I just...we're on the same page about the relationship. We love each other. We want to be together for the long haul. We rarely fight, right?"

"Right." Alex's tone had a hint of skepticism. "What are you getting at, Nicholas?"

"If the wedding is the problem...let's just...not."

"Not what?"

"Not get married. Let's forget the whole thing and just be together. Do we actually need the wedding to be in love? No, clearly not. All it's done is brought us frustration. So...no wedding."

"You don't mean that."

"I do. If that's what's hurting us, we won't get married."

Alex studied Nicholas's face. Nicholas stood there as he watched Alex process, watched the thoughts go through his head. "So that's it, then? We're cancelling an entire wedding because I missed an email?"

Nicholas pulled on his hair and resisted the urge to shake Alex. "No! Not because of an email. Jeez, Alex. Do you really think I'd be this upset about one email?"

Alex blinked back tears that were so evident Nicholas could see them. "I don't know!" he shot back. "Ever since we started planning this wedding, I've been sitting here stressing about how we could pull it off without frustration. I've been concerned that we're making it such a production. *You've* been stressed that it isn't going exactly how you planned, even though every time we start to make a decision, you go another way. And now your solution is to not marry each other at all because I missed a freaking email. That's the straw that broke the camel's back for you? Not me pleading with you to elope so we could avoid all this drama? Now, when it's your photo shoot, you want us to call it all off?"

Nicholas could hear the ache in Alex's voice, as the words sank in. Selfish. Self-focused. His head up his own ass, really. Not Alex—of course not—but Nicholas himself. He reached for Alex, and his heart dropped when Alex tugged back before giving in and hugging him. "It was an accident," Alex mumbled against his shoulder.

"I know," Nicholas said. "I'm not saying we should call it off because I don't love you. Obviously, I love you. But maybe now is the wrong time."

Alex pulled back. "For just the wedding, right?"

Nicholas nodded. "Just the wedding. Maybe we need to focus on rebuilding after the fire before we make any massive decisions or have a giant wedding. Maybe cancel is the wrong word. Maybe we need to postpone. Indefinitely." His throat tightened and he struggled to get out the words.

"For clarification, you're saying you want to be with me. You just don't want to marry me. Right now. Or maybe ever. But especially now?" Alex asked.

"I do want to marry you. But I don't want to keep fighting over details again and again and again until we're both blue in the face, and we're clearly both very distracted with the fire and we can't agree on any of the details in the first place," Nicholas said, rushing the words together all at once. "It's not about our relationship being in trouble in any way. It's about making sure it doesn't *get* in trouble when we're not even on the same page."

Alex nodded and took it in, curling into him. "If we can't decide on a wedding, though...what does that mean for us?"

"I think it just means we have different ideas on weddings."

"Yeah. I guess."

The sadness in his tone, the skepticism, was like a stake in Nicholas's heart. Nothing he said in the moment would convince Alex this was okay, nor would it convince him it wasn't about the photos specifically. There was no going back and saying, "You know what? Never mind." Or maybe there was, but Nicholas wasn't sure he could turn around and do that when they were both clearly aching from what they'd said and how they were around each other right now.

*

"Wait, you're doing *what?*" Jade asked. "You're joking." The shock in her voice from the other room made it clear what he was telling her.

Alex walked in, tugging his T-shirt down with one hand, towel-drying his hair with the other.

"For now, Jade. Not forever," Nicholas explained. Alex studied the look on her face, the way she was gripping the counter, and he watched her shrug. Clearly, she was trying to pass it off as less of a big deal than it was.

Alex understood that. He didn't feel good about it either. "With the fire and stuff, we decided we needed to focus on getting our lives back on track before we add more to that list." He felt sick saying it. Ever since they'd called off the wedding the day before, they'd been okay, but tense. Nicholas still held him while he slept at night and made toaster pastries for breakfast, but Alex wondered if that was more because baking calmed his nerves, and his body was simply used to holding him.

Things weren't normal and okay, as much as they wanted to believe they could be. And even if this was the right choice, it certainly wasn't an easy one. Alex didn't want to be at arm's length from his fiancé besides when they cuddled in bed. And after twenty-four hours, he was starting to wonder if they were both kidding themselves into thinking things would work out, or if they'd recover from this argument the way he wanted them to.

"That makes sense," Jade said, voice tense. "Why not postpone instead of cancelling?"

"We are, kind of," Nicholas answered. "We're going to get married. We didn't call off our engagement. We just didn't think setting a new date made sense in case we had to postpone that too."

Alex froze in place. Was that what they were doing? He looked Nicholas in the eyes. Were they staving off the inevitable, some grand realization they'd never actually get married? Alex was worried that was the case, and he wasn't okay with that. He needed to change his mind and get on board with a big wedding—and fast. He'd rather sacrifice a day of headaches for a lifetime of happiness with Nicholas.

"Worst case scenario, we could always do a courthouse wedding and have a reception another time," Nicholas added, and Alex wondered if he was feeling okay. In what universe would Nicholas offer up a courthouse wedding? Alex had no idea.

Jade shook her head. "Right, I mean... I guess whatever works for you two. It's your wedd—er...lack of wedding. So long as you both are happy, we're happy with whatever you do." She reached forward and tugged Nicholas into a hug. As much as Alex wanted a hug, too, he was worried it would only break the carefully crafted dam barely containing his emotions. There had to be a compromise to be reached, a realization they were at their breaking point, the moment of "go big or go home" that Alex had desperately wanted to go home from.

And now, all he wanted was to be married to Nicholas. Nicholas was a dream, wedding aside. He was everything Alex had ever hoped for, dreamed of meeting, and the obsessive need for a giant wedding was one of the few flaws Alex could hold against him. And that wasn't Nicholas's fault. It was a conflict of personalities, a butting of heads they couldn't seem to get past. Alex was bound and determined to get past it. He didn't want to walk on eggshells forever, and they needed to talk, to see what the plan was. Was there a future for them? Alex was certain there was, beyond the wedding drama.

He excused himself to the bedroom, as if he was still getting ready for the day, and he could hear Nicholas telling Jade all about job applications, and how postponing the wedding would really give him time to settle into a stable new job after his fellowship ended. He knew that wasn't what Nicholas was postponing for.

As he sat on the edge of the bed, rubbing lotion on his heels, he considered why he was so opposed to the large wedding. Much of his hesitation came from the sheer number of details, the commitment to a million moving cogs. That spelled headache to him. He'd come to terms with it in a lot of ways though. As he'd worked on a wedding binder for Nicholas, he'd at least started to see the vision he had for it. He could *almost* understand the appeal, in spite of the thought that a wedding so grand made him itch with worry something would go wrong.

Maybe he needed to sit Nicholas down, demand a compromise, and say he wanted to have the dream wedding, but on a slightly smaller scale. He meant what he said when they were arguing: He wasn't sure the wedding Nicholas was planning was rooted in what he wanted, as much as it stemmed from a sense of nostalgia and security. He'd only realized that when they'd rearranged the furniture in the new apartment the weekend before. He had an itch to arrange the living room exactly as it had sat in the old apartment, but then realized with different furniture and a different apartment, trying to make those pieces fit into his new life in the same way didn't work. He wondered if this was much the same for Nicholas, if he was trying to take the pieces of a life he'd dreamed of when his mother was alive, one that felt safe and made him feel like he had a life no matter what happened to her, and was trying to fit them in this life, a decade later.

But he wasn't sure Nicholas could see that. So, he resigned himself to the one thing he knew would work, the phone call that would prove to Nicholas he wanted this wedding to happen, and not just someday, but on the timeline they'd planned. He grabbed a business card out of a side table drawer, one he hadn't yet pasted into the new binder, and dialed the number.

"Hi. Is this Alyssa?" he asked. "It's Alex Ross. I was calling to reschedule that photography session."

Chapter Seventeen

The Art of the Apology

Nicholas rolled out a pie crust on the floured countertop and tried to keep his breathing calm and even. When Alex had disappeared into the bedroom, he'd assumed he was only getting ready and would pop back out, but even after Jade waited ten minutes to tell him goodbye, he hadn't reappeared. She'd left, and now he was alone with his thoughts, rolling out pie crust and cutting it into rectangles.

"What are you doing?" he asked himself. "He's in there. Go talk to him." Nicholas knew they needed to talk. They'd danced around the subject every time it almost got brought up, and instead of talking about it, they'd watched movies. Alex had rejected his offer for a blanket fort, and Nicholas had rejected Alex's offer of a shower. Clearly, they both wanted to make amends for their argument, but also didn't want to let the other in at all.

Deep down, Nicholas knew he was being stubborn. Was he so unwilling to budge on a disagreement like this, the final hill for them to cross to becoming husband and husband? No, he didn't think so, but a nagging voice in the back of his head said that if Alex couldn't accept his dream wedding, then maybe Alex couldn't accept Nicholas. Nicholas *was* over the top. His friends called him extra for a reason. In the core of his being, he'd always been a little bit extreme, from baking for his entire hall to driving hours for an ingredient for a recipe his grandmother wanted to make. He'd always gone to extremes when he had his mind set on something. This was no exception.

In fact, this was the one place he didn't feel should *be* an exception.

Nicholas was over the top, weddings were over the top, and Nicholas having an over-the-top wedding was exactly what people would expect of him. His mother knew that was what he wanted. His friends knew. So why couldn't he get his fiancé on board? Maybe he needed to dismiss the idea of a wedding altogether. A part of his mind tingled at the idea of Alex being right after all.

Was Nicholas planning a big wedding because he wanted a big wedding? He wasn't sure. Every time Alex called out the fact that the bigger they made their wedding, the more things could go wrong, Nicholas felt a twinge of fear. Alex was right. How could he avoid that string of worry, that fear of something going wrong, and instead of him enjoying his wedding day, he'd be singularly focused on the aspects that were failing?

Ever since the fire, and then the photographer situation, he'd struggled to see another way around it. A wedding, he realized, meant certain parts were bound to go wrong. Rather than face that reality, Nicholas thought calling it off would be right. As he spooned filling onto the rectangles he cut, he started to realize that his decision to call off the wedding had far less to do with Alex's criticisms of it, and everything to do with his own fears. He simply hadn't considered that as the reason until this moment, as he thought through what else could go wrong.

"Alex?" he called, pressing rectangles of pie crust over the filling.

Alex poked his head out of the door, eyes tired like they'd been since the last time they talked about this the night before. *Really* talked about this. "What's up?"

"I—" As Nicholas looked at Alex, he started to chicken out. They'd already decided to postpone, so why discuss it now? Nicholas bit his lip and then released it. "I wanted to know if you wanted me to frost these or not." He glanced down at the pastries he was getting ready to put in the oven.

"Oh. Yeah, um. Why not frost half and leave the other half? Then we don't have to decide." His crestfallen face only added to Nicholas's feelings of guilt. "I think I'm going to go for a drive."

"Want me to come with?"

"Nah, I just wanted to go get gas so I wouldn't have to wake up so early tomorrow before work," Alex said softly.

Another lie. Their miscommunications, their great divide, looked worse than ever, but Nicholas wasn't ready to talk about it. He wasn't ready to admit that he'd been wrong in the situation, or that Alex knew him too well. "Okay. If I'm not here when you get back, I'm running to the store after this. Need anything?"

Alex shrugged. "I think we're out of popcorn. We were going to watch a movie tonight, right?"

Nicholas nodded. "Popcorn. Got it." At least they were still on for movie night. Some things hadn't changed.

*

Nicholas needed advice. Real-life, "am I being unreasonable?" kind of advice from someone who was married and knew better. Ever since she left the other day, Nicholas wondered why he hadn't taken the opportunity to pick Jade's brain, to ask if she or Veronica had disagreed on the plan to elope, or if they were both on board. He wished he had asked her how to apologize for a fight this big. He and Alex had argued, but they'd never been this far from seeing eye to eye on something. Not since before they really got to know each other, at least.

When Nicholas pulled into the parking lot in front of Jade's, which he wasn't allowing himself to think of as home anymore because it hurt too much, Alex's car was in the parking lot too. "For someone who claims to not be sentimental..." Of *course,* Alex would be sitting outside the old apartment. They hadn't gone back inside after the time they'd said goodbye, in part because it had been locked for repairs and renovations. The apartment didn't belong to them anymore, and they'd had good timing to say goodbye to it when they did. That hadn't stopped Alex from going over there. Nicholas knew he'd been stopping by, mostly because he'd driven there a few times out of habit on his way home, going to the wrong home after work and realizing as he pulled up out front. He hadn't asked Alex about it, not wanting to call him out, but he knew a lot of Alex working late was Alex being here.

Nicholas got out of the car and walked inside and past Jade's apartment to their old one. Alex was nowhere to be seen. He tried the doorknob. Nothing. Brows furrowed, he looked around the hallway. Had he missed him? Maybe. He could have come up in the elevator while Alex took the stairs down. Nicholas shook his head and headed for Jade's, the plan he'd had to begin with.

He knocked on the door and started to open it, their usual open-door policy in place, but Jade stood in the doorway. "Hey, Nicholas. What's up?" She barely had the door cracked open at all.

"You okay?" Nicholas asked.

"Ye-uh, yeah," Jade said.

"Blink twice if you're in danger?"

Jade smirked and glanced back into the apartment.

"Should I come back later?"

"No, uh. Um..." She sighed. "Sorry, Alex," she said, swinging the door open. Alex was seated at the table, a stack of magazines beside him and a glue stick in his hand. He looked guilty as sin, face flushed and eyes wide. He looked away from Nicholas as if avoiding eye contact would make it better.

"Hey," Nicholas said, walking in and giving Jade's arm a gentle squeeze as he headed into the kitchen and sat down at the table. "I thought you were at the apartment." He smirked slightly, mostly because Alex looked like he was in deep trouble and Nicholas wanted to set his mind at ease. Reaching for Alex's hand, he glanced at the magazines. He could tell what they were right away.

"I'm...not, clearly," Alex whispered, looking at the binder more than Nicholas. He didn't move his hand.

"Can I see?" Nicholas asked, reaching forward for the binder.

Alex nodded and shoved it toward him, capping the glue stick. "Yeah. Sure."

Nicholas looked at the page and then flipped to a few other pages. "This...is a wedding binder."

"Yeah."

"You've been making a wedding binder?" He turned back to the first page and scanned it. It looked familiar. Not quite like his old one, of course, but it had the same sense of his style and taste. He turned the next page. Every page was laid out like his. Nothing was exact, but Alex hadn't looked at the binder the number of times Nicholas had. The binder held all the features though. The checklists of what to do at each step before the wedding, some website listings, the colors and tuxedos and other signatures of the wedding Nicholas had picked out. Nicholas, as much as he was smiling about how well Alex knew him, felt nerves getting the best of him as he flipped through the pages. "This is beautiful, Alex," he said, tears in his eyes.

"I know it isn't the one you and your mom started, but—"

"You did a really good job." His tears spilled over now as he kept turning pages, looking at the carefully added tabbed dividers and the pictures and the notes.

"You're not happy with it," Alex noted. Despite Nicholas's smile and his attempt to pass off his tears as tears of joy and appreciation, Alex knew him too well. "What did I get wrong? I can...I can fix it." Alex held up his glue stick.

Nicholas pulled Alex's hand to his lips and kissed his knuckles, meeting his eyes and swiping at his tears so he could see Alex properly. "This isn't the wedding you want. It's the wedding I wa—thought I wanted."

"Hey, V, I think it's time for us to go to the gym, yeah?" Jade piped in from across the room.

"But—"

"Veronica, please. Gym. Let's go," Jade urged.

"I'm not dres—"

Nicholas looked up in time to see Jade tugging Veronica's arm and pulling her to the door, mumbling a little too loudly, "We're not actually going to the gym. They need time alone."

Veronica shook her head in protest. "But it's our apartment!" she stage-whispered.

"I don't care. Come *on*."

Nicholas would have to remember to thank them both later. Alex cocked his head to one side. "I don't understand. I tried to get it exactly how you had it before and I rebooked the engagement shoot, which was supposed to be a surprise to you, and—"

Nicholas leaned in and kissed Alex gently. "Alex? Sweetheart, I love you. *Shhh*, just for two seconds. Let me explain." He ran his fingers through Alex's hair and pressed their foreheads together as he considered how to explain. "I thought that a big grand wedding was the only real option. I mean, you know how I am about going over the top. But you're right. I wanted to tell you earlier, but I didn't...I didn't want to say you were right, I guess," Nicholas said, blushing. "If anything, I thought maybe if I were stubborn enough, I could change my whole nature, but you had me pegged. If anything went wrong, even the smallest detail, I would be more focused on that than on our wedding and the fact that I get to marry you. And I proved that, didn't I? I let the little stuff, like the photo shoot, get under my skin until I exploded. I don't want a wedding like that!" Alex started to say something, but Nicholas held his finger up to his lips. "I wanted this wedding because I'd spent a decade thinking I wanted this wedding, but when I look it over, I see it in front of my face after not looking at it for a few weeks and I think...what am I trying to prove? Who am I trying to be?"

Alex nodded and pulled back from Nicholas's finger. "So, what does that mean, then?"

"It means this binder is beautiful. and I am going to treasure it for all the work you put into it, because this is one of the nicest things anyone has ever done for me. This ranks higher than your apology snowman, and it makes me smile that you go so far out of your way to apologize to me in ways that you *know* will make me tear up. And it also means we're getting a new binder and planning a new wedding...one we both want. Does that sound okay? Because I can give up the giant three-ring circus, but I cannot give up the organized binder. Sorry. That's just...not happening." Nicholas laughed, swiping at one of Alex's tears and kissing him again. "Alex, will you marry me?"

Alex beamed and nodded and kissed Nicholas again, arms around him tightly, and Nicholas had no doubts at all about how they would move forward. He was ready to compromise, ready to plan the wedding of their dreams, not only his, and he could feel Alex's heart beating against his hand as he clung to him, kissing his neck and his jaw with small, quick pecks.

"So, I take it the wedding is back on?" Jade asked, and Nicholas jerked away from Alex.

He nodded. "Yeah, it is."

"I wasn't eavesdropping. I forgot my phone."

Nicholas quirked a brow and tilted his head to one side.

"Okay, fine," Jade confessed. "I was eavesdropping."

Alex laughed and stood up, hugging her. "I think as our officiant, you're allowed to eavesdrop." He turned back to Nicholas and Nicholas looked at him, eyes bright and happier than he'd seen Alex in days. "So, we need popcorn *and* a binder, huh?"

Chapter Eighteen

Back On

Alex liked wedding planning. He hadn't expected to, but as he scrolled through a website searching for ideas, he realized how much he did actually like it. "Look," he said, lifting his laptop over a pillow to Nicholas. "We should do this."

He watched Nicholas's face as he studied the screen, and when Nicholas smiled, Alex took that as a yes. "I know your family has passed but it doesn't mean we can't honor them," he said softly, and Nicholas nodded in response. Alex bookmarked the idea for them to return to, a simple sign reserving seats for those who couldn't be there because they'd passed away. The gesture was a small one, but it would mean a lot to Nicholas and Alex knew that.

"I love that idea," he answered.

He closed his laptop and gazed up at the sheets above him, tacked to the walls in their first blanket fort since the fire. "How are we getting so much done? The first time around, we barely checked anything off in months, but it's only taken us a weekend to plan it again."

"Because we both love the plan this time," Nicholas said, closing his binder and climbing onto Alex, nuzzling at his nose, a sweet bunny kiss. "Because it's the wedding we're supposed to be having this time."

Alex beamed. "You're right. It's going to be a dream wedding, isn't it?" He tugged Nicholas down in a kiss, which he smiled into.

"It is," Nicholas agreed when he pulled back. "And you're going to look so, so hot in that tux." He grazed a hand up Alex's side.

Alex curled into his touch and laughed, kicking at him and trying to wriggle away from the ticklish feeling. "We'll both be hot."

Nicholas rolled off him and went back to the magazine he'd been looking through. "What do you think of pie?"

"In general, or...?" Alex snorted. "Pie is good. Unique. Kind of rustic." He opened his laptop and searched. "I think we could do pie, but you'd probably end up having to make them because I think you'll end up criticizing every baker in town on their crust."

"Jade said the same thing!"

"If it's true, it's true. We know you. Nobody will get it flaky like you do." He turned the computer toward Nicholas. "What if we do these?" They were little single-serving pies in a jar, a lid on top and a wooden fork tied to each, with cute, printed labels of the flavor pasted on the side. "Then we could mix and match and people who didn't want them right then could take them home to enjoy later. Or we could plan two for each person, one for the wedding and one for home."

"What about a cake cutting though?" Nicholas asked.

"So, you and I get a regular pie to cut into then," he shrugged. "Except no face smashing. If you reveal the fact that I'm wearing concealer, I'm saying it's grounds for divorce." He pulled Nicholas in for another kiss, and this time, they had both forgotten planning altogether, with Nicholas shifting back onto him and kissing him languidly, nice and slow and soft.

"Already planning our divorce, huh?"

"Only if you reveal my makeup. You know that's my little secret."

Nicholas kissed him again. "Okay. No face smashes. No concealer reveals. Promise."

Alex giggled when Nicholas's beard got to his neck. Even after all this time, it tickled when Nicholas kissed him, tickled in the best ways, tickled in ways that got him turned on and worked up. He tilted his head back to give Nicholas more space, letting Nicholas kiss down his neck and slide his shirt up so he could kiss his nipples too. "Feels nice," Alex mumbled, eyes slipping closed so he could enjoy this fully. When Nicholas grazed his fingers on the other side, opposite his mouth, it elicited a moan from Alex, and a lip bite.

Nicholas kept working his way down Alex's body, kisses down his abdomen before he dipped his tongue into Alex's belly button. "Oh, gosh..." Alex whimpered. "Are we planning the wedding or the honey—*mmph*—honeymoon?" He arched his back.

"Both," Nicholas said, hands on Alex's waistband, sliding his pants down. "I think it's good to be prepared for both aspects of our upcoming matrimony."

Alex smiled, arching his back and letting Nicholas work his magic. Nicholas always knew the ways to get him going, and he slipped his hands under Alex, grasping his ass as he took him into his mouth, going deeper right away and pulling off with a subtle *pop*. Alex teased his fingers through Nicholas's hair, watching him as he went down on him, tongue running along the length.

And then the phone rang, jerking Nicholas's head up and snapping the fibers of the impromptu intimate moment. "Ignore it," Nicholas said, but Alex was already moving toward it.

"Might be the photographer," he mentioned, answering. "Hello?" He'd reached for it so fast that when he stood, he hadn't fully gotten his pants back up. His pajama shorts hung around his knees and he tugged at them with one hand to get them back up, even as Nicholas crawled across the floor to him and knelt in front of him. Focusing on the phone call was difficult.

Alex glanced down at Nicholas. "Can we do ten in the morning tomorrow?" he asked.

"Of course," Nicholas said.

Alex parroted that back into the phone. As the photographer explained details—what colors to wear, what to bring, how long the session was—Alex reached for a notepad and scribbled it down. Or, he attempted to, because Nicholas was running his hands up his thighs and it was very, very distracting. As Alex tried to take down the address, he had to ask them to repeat it three times because Nicholas was stroking him gently. "Thanks!" he squeaked. "See you tomorrow."

As soon as he hung up the phone he was moving, pushing Nicholas backward gently onto the floor. "I can't believe you were trying to distract me while I was on the phone!" he said, yelping as he toppled onto Nicholas, kissing him and working his way down Nicholas as payback. "You, sir, are naughty, and I think you're a bad influence."

Nicholas laughed hard enough that his stomach rippled with the sound, and Alex kissed him there, watching the way his body moved in the moment. "I'm sure you got all of the important details," he said, dismissing Alex's concern with a wave.

"Sure. I was very focused on that phone call. Just remember if it goes wrong this time, *you* were the distraction."

Nicholas laughed harder and tugged Alex back up for a kiss. Right when Alex's hand found Nicholas's length and began to stroke, the phone rang again.

Nicholas glanced at the caller ID. "I think that's a sign we should stop. It's your mother."

Alex sighed and sat on the floor, back against the couch. "Hey, Mom," he said. *Way to kill the mood, Mom.*

Chapter Nineteen

Pride

Alex and his mother had come a long way in a year and a half. Nicholas had heard the stories and the frustration Alex had about his gap year, taking a year off to tend to his mother as she started therapy and dealt with her depression in the wake of her divorce. Nicholas always considered it a chicken and egg situation. He wasn't sure if the depression played a role in the divorce or the divorce played a role in the depression or both or neither, and they were just two separate events in her life.

Not that it mattered—both of these things affected her deeply, and by extension, they affected Alex.

What *did* matter was that Alex and his mother were communicating better now—or mostly. She'd waned off on her support when "I'm gay" turned into "I met someone and it's serious," but she always put on a happy face regardless. Alex hadn't given up, though, and his mother had opened up more in therapy and talked to him about his sexuality. Now, they talked on the phone several times a week to catch up. Nicholas was happy with that.

He was less happy about it interrupting what they'd been doing, but the intimate moment could wait. "Yeah, Mom. The wedding is back on." Nicholas overheard him talking to her from the bedroom as he paced back and forth around their bed. Nicholas stayed cozy in the fort, tearing out magazine pages with the perfect country-meets-city-chic style. It represented them. Not that Nicholas was country, but they had a Midwest-meets-LA love story, and that was good enough for their varied tastes. "I'm just glad you kept your ticket... Yeah, it would have been great to see you that weekend even if there weren't a wedding."

Nicholas knew Alex missed his mother too. They'd been able to visit her exactly once. But a part of Nicholas ached. The ache wasn't jealousy, per se. It wasn't as if he wanted Alex to not have a mom so he would understand the pain Nicholas felt in losing his. No, he wished he could be doing what Alex was doing right now. Talking to his mother, telling her all about the wedding and the plans they had. As he listened to Alex detail the wedding theme and the colors and their updated registry and the engagement photos they were doing, Nicholas longed to do the same.

Instead, he stood up, and he walked into the kitchen. As he pulled out a rolling pin and wished it had the same weight as the one he'd gotten from his mother, he gave it a small spin. Hers had been a heavy wood, solid, with a slight squeak as it moved. This one was stainless steel with red handles, no squeak, and the handles weren't centered in the roller, designed to be ergonomic, but taking away the character completely. There was no replacing his mother's rolling pin. There was no filling the hole in his heart losing his mother had left.

"Hey, Ma," he whispered into the quiet kitchen. He pulled her recipes down from the shelf. Though he'd once been upset Alex had saved these, which were backed up on the computer, instead of the binder, now he was thankful. Scans wouldn't have picked up the full detail. Scrawls of recipes he'd worked on with his mother—her handwriting overlapping her mother's, with his notes in the margins too. He shuffled around in the freezer and pulled out a bag of frozen strawberries intended for morning smoothies. He'd have to replace their smoothie stock later. Now, he needed his mom.

He checked for the other ingredients, thrilled they had almost everything he needed. It was all earmarked for other meals: pretzels for sack lunches at work, cream cheese for a spaghetti recipe he'd been meaning to try, sugar as an ever-present fixture of his kitchen counters. It would work.

"I'm getting married, Ma," Nicholas said, rolling a rolling pin over a Ziploc bag of pretzels. "He's the most incredible guy I've ever met. He understands me." A tear fell from his eye onto his hand. "He's handsome. Red hair, a little scruff, the whole nine yards."

He poured the crushed pretzels into a bowl and started to heat butter, glancing at the recipe he had made so many times he knew it by heart. "It's been crazy planning the wedding. Alex burned the wedding binder, but he didn't mean to." He kept mumbling to himself as he mixed the butter onto the pretzels. "We had all these plans, Momma. You and me. We thought we knew what it would be like. Remember when I made you that wedding cake sample?" Nicholas listened to the answering silence, and for a moment, he wondered if he was insane to be talking to his deceased mom in the middle of an empty kitchen. Still, he couldn't help himself. "Turns out we're probably going to have pie instead. Oh well. You knew what my pies tasted like." He smiled to himself.

"It's funny, because I'm not upset that we changed plans. I thought I would be, but I'm not. My taste has changed a lot since I was sixteen. I like really different things now. So, uh. I guess my only real regret is that you're not going to get to see what it's like now. That you're not getting to see what *I'm* like now." He choked on the tears that were falling from his eyes. He placed the pan in the oven to bake the pretzel crust and then turned his attention to the cream cheese, beating it with sugar. "I really hope you'd be proud of me, Mama." As he folded in whipped topping, he smiled. "I think you would have been."

Nicholas turned most of his attention to the recipe, spreading the cream cheese mixture onto the pretzels. He kept talking. "I applied to some jobs, Mom. I don't think I'm going to get any of them, but I did apply. I've been thinking if I don't find the right software engineering job, I'll try for a teaching position, since the fellowship has gone so well." He paced the kitchen, walking between the crust and the cabinet, the freezer and the countertop. "You always told me I'd make a good teacher. And I do like working as a teaching fellow, but... I don't know." He talked to her as if she existed in the space in the kitchen, because in many ways, she did. Nicholas and his mother spent much of their time together in the kitchen, so remembering her there was easier than remembering her anywhere else.

He thumbed over the recipe and her notes in the margin. "Nobody thinks I'll be able to order bakery pies for the wedding. Not without worrying about the crust," he said, tearing up. "If they'd have learned your tips for a flakier crust, it wouldn't be an issue, would it?" Part of him waited for her to answer. He could still hear her voice, soft and deep like she'd just swallowed a spoonful of honey. "Sometimes I worry I'm too high maintenance," he confessed. "I mean, the crusts are an obvious example, but what about calling off the entire dang wedding because I was upset about some photos?" He shook his head and mixed the gelatin, adding in the frozen strawberries. "You didn't raise me to be like that. Not really." He paused as he thought about it. "Or maybe you did."

He recalled the time his mother had sewn him a cape because none of the store ones fit his long, lanky figure, and she told him, "If no one else can do it right, then you learn to do it right yourself." The stores hadn't exactly done it wrong. They'd gone for the common sizes, the kids who were shorter than him. No one had intended to make a cape that only fit down to his butt, but they had. And the lesson had stuck with him: If no one else could do what was necessary to get the job done the way he needed it to be, he'd do the work himself. So, he strode across the room, walking to the binder they'd been working on together, and opened to the dessert tab. In the margin, he wrote *ask if they use vodka in their crust*. If none of the bakeries did, he'd make the pies himself.

"Thanks, Mom," he said, pouring the strawberries and gelatin over the cream cheese mixture and placing the whole dish in the fridge. As he filed the recipe away, he smiled to himself and wiped the tears from his eyes. "You always know how to make it better."

Chapter Twenty

Singin' in the Rain

Alex straightened his shirt again. "Are you sure this is the right shirt?" he asked, tugging at the hem.

"It looks perfect," Nicholas said, kissing him. "The color looks so good with your hair."

Alex practically preened at the way Nicholas ran his hand through his hair and then interlaced their fingers right after. "Let's go. We can't miss the shoot this time." They'd been counting the days for the do-over photo shoot, the chance to try again after missing the first one entirely. Alex was nervous, to say the least.

"I hate having my picture taken," Alex admitted. "I always look so awkward."

"Then don't. Don't look awkward, ignore the camera, and focus on me instead." Alex snorted in response. Nicholas clarified, "Okay, I'm not being egotistical if it's a photo shoot for us together. We're supposed to be focused on each other, goofball." He shoved Alex's shoulder with his and Alex beamed.

"Okay. I'll focus on you." That was a relief, actually, the idea he'd be focused on Nicholas and not the camera in front of him.

Nicholas had come up with the perfect idea, a *Singin' in the Rain* photo shoot, with spotted umbrellas. Rain had fallen earlier that morning, and on seeing the forecast their wedding photographer had rescheduled the shoot by a day, just to give them authentic puddles instead of homemade ones. Nicholas had searched for the perfect brightly colored boots and found them, so Alex wore blue rain boots and a yellow shirt, and Nicholas wore yellow rain boots and a blue shirt. The umbrella? Yellow-and-blue spots all over it, at Nicholas's request. Alex had scoured the internet for it, and when he found exactly what he'd been looking for, he'd been ecstatic.

Alex couldn't get over how attractive Nicholas was in the outfit, and he only hoped that Nicholas felt the same about him. Based on how Nicholas could barely keep his eyes off Alex on the drive over, he got the impression the feeling was mutual, and Alex beamed with pride and happiness. "I'm actually excited," he admitted as they got closer, pulling into the parking lot of the address they'd been given, on the edge of a nearby farm.

The concrete parking lot was full of little dips, each one filled with water from the recent rain, puddles covering various stretches of the surface. A field of wildflowers stretched out behind them, some small and demure and others tall and facing the light. So many of them were the same shades of blue and yellow Nicholas and Alex wore, which made him smile. The sky was a blissful blue with rays of sunlight peeking out behind white puffy clouds. Beside them, a red, weathered barn stood firm, with a silo stretching up high beside it. As Alex scanned the area, he realized how perfect it would look with their bright clothes, the cerulean and sun attire they had on. "I love it," Alex said. When they'd discussed the shoot being on a farm, Alex worried it would remind him too much of his grandfather's. He was wrong; this was such a different farm, a different experience. Here, he was happy.

The photographer pulled up beside them. "Oh, you look cute!" she called from her open car window. "Give me five minutes to get my equipment together, and then we'll be all set." She seemed nice. That was at least a little reassuring.

Alex turned toward Nicholas and hooked their pinkies together, looking up at him and studying his face. "I'm really glad we're doing this," he said. Nicholas grazed his cheek with his fingertips and kissed him, Alex's chin tilted up like a sunflower attracted to the sun.

"I'm glad too," Nicholas answered. "Thank you for rescheduling it." He ran his thumb over Alex's lower lip, tugging it out into a pout as he smiled wide, cheeks rosy and puffed up over his beard. Alex loved when Nicholas smiled like that. It reached his eyes and lit up his whole face, a genuine expression that he couldn't contain. When Nicholas smiled like that, he was elated, not just happy, and nothing pleased Alex more than being the cause.

Focused entirely on Nicholas, Alex kept holding him close, a hand in Nicholas's back pocket and the umbrella hooked on his wrist as he kissed him again. They had time, waiting for the photographer to get her equipment ready and sort out the precise location of the first few shots, so Alex wasn't even paying much attention to anything but

Nicholas. He tugged at his beard gently, kissing him at the corner of his lips. As he heard the shutter click, it occurred to them that their photographer was ready—she simply hadn't told them yet. He smirked. *Good.* Alex liked the idea of candid shots of them together far more than the staged, posed shots Nicholas had prepared him for.

After several minutes, she walked over to them. "How about we go find a good puddle to jump in?"

By the end of an hour, Alex's ankles were covered in mud, his jeans soaking wet. His legs ached from posing, the kneeling and jumping into puddles, the walking to get just the right angle. Sinking into the car after the shoot, he held Nicholas's hand, blinking at him with tired, but still bright eyes. "I'm so glad we did that."

"Me too. How about we go home and have some dessert and cuddle?" Nicholas leaned across the space between them and kissed his cheek. "I love you."

Alex smiled. "Better we get dessert than something savory, because you're cheesy enough," he teased. "I love you too. Now watch the road." He stared ahead at the road, a few wildflowers resting on the dashboard of the car in the corner of his vision. Nicholas planned to press them when they got home, an everlasting memory of their pictures.

"I'm thinking wildflowers for the wedding," Nicholas said after a long stretch of comfortable silence.

"Funny, because I was thinking the same thing."

Chapter Twenty-One

Nicholas's Secret

Secrets were not Nicholas's forte at all. Maybe that was why he'd come out to his mom two days after he'd gotten his first crush. He couldn't keep it a secret, couldn't resist telling her right away. His inability to keep secrets was also why Jade knew instantaneously about his love for redheads and boys who wore beanies. But this—the one he had right now—was a bigger secret, and he was keeping it from more people than just Jade. He sat on the couch and tried to wait for Alex to get home from work.

When that made him too restless, he got up and cleaned the kitchen, trying to distract himself. He almost laughed. That was more of an Alex thing to do than something he would have done, which should have told him what he needed to know about how nervous he was right then. He paced back and forth and eventually started making the crust for his beefy potato taco pie for their potluck dinner that night if only to get his mind off everything. He was stressed, to say the least. What would Alex even say to his secret? Would he be thrilled? Would he be upset?

Maybe he wouldn't be either one.

Nicholas also considered Jade's reaction; hers was contingent on Alex's reaction. If he was hesitant, Jade would hesitate. If he was thrilled, she'd suck up any worry she had and be thrilled for both of them. She would have been more contingent on Nicholas's reaction, but obviously, he'd applied for the job and was excited about it, despite his nerves. Nicholas bit his lip and rolled out the pastry. "If it gets the right thickness as I push forward, he'll be excited, and if it gets to the right thickness when I pull back, he'll hate it," Nicholas said to himself. He rolled out the bottom crust, pushing the rolling pin back and forth until he had it where he wanted it. "He's going to hate it," he said. As he rolled the top crust after, his last push was forward. "Okay, well, maybe he'll love it." He shook his head. "I don't know."

Putting on some music, he thought, might help him get out of his head; he turned it loud, to some acoustic pop station playing "I'm Yours." He scrolled down and added it to the playlist of possible wedding songs. "Okay. Just...don't think about it," he said, singing louder as he diced potatoes. The louder he sang, the less he worried, and eventually the tension had melted off him.

"Hey," Alex said, jarring him from his thoughts. "I'm not drunk and it's not Christmas, so I guess I'll let the loud music slide," he joked, kissing his shoulder. "Working on dinner?"

Nicholas nodded, biting his lip. Should he tell him now? Wait until he was done? Either way, he had to tell him before dinner. He glanced at the pie and glanced back at Alex. "How was work?"

"Good," he said. "About that, actually..." Alex grinned wide and put his hands on the counter. "Guess who got offered a promotion to assistant manager today?"

"Are you serious?" Nicholas asked, reaching forward and hugging him, trying not to get flour on his shirt. "I'm so proud of you." Now, Nicholas felt bad for the news he had to give him. This time, his secret would force Alex to choose more than he already had to. "How's that going to work with school?"

Alex shrugged. "I'm almost done, so it shouldn't overlap too much. I figure it gives me something to do until graduation." Alex was inching closer and closer to graduation, and Nicholas chalked that up as another reason he shouldn't take the job.

"That's, uh, that's great, sweetheart. I'm really, really happy for you." He hugged him again and returned to stirring the ground beef on the stove.

"Thanks. So, you going to tell me what's with the music today?" Alex asked, hopping up on the counter and swinging his legs.

"It's not important," Nicholas hedged. The last thing he wanted to do was steal Alex's thunder, especially when Alex seemed so happy with this development, his promotion and the future here in Omaha.

"Nicholas, talk to me." Alex grasped his arm. "What's going on?"

"I got some news today, too, that's all." Nicholas turned his attention to the ground beef on the stove.

"What kind of news?"

Nicholas wiped his hands on a rag tucked over the stove handle and turned back toward his music. He turned it off and looked at Alex, stepping between his legs and resting his hands on his thighs. With Alex on the counter, they were almost the same height. Not quite, but close. "I got a job offer."

"Oh my gosh, are you serious?" Alex asked. "Which one?"

Nicholas had applied to countless jobs, and after a while he stopped telling Alex which ones he was trying for because there'd been so many. He'd had a few interviews, and a few video calls. He took a deep breath. "A software engineering job...at Garmin." A job at Garmin meant a move south, a new home, three hours away from where they were now. "I'm going to turn it down," he added.

"Are you kidding me? Why would you turn that down?" Alex asked, eyes wide and grabbing his shoulders. "Baby, you gotta take it. That's your dream!"

"You just got a promotion, and we're happy in Omaha. We're happy here. We have a wedding here in less than a year, and everything planned out and—"

"And? Nicholas, take the job. It's the one you want. I'll apply at another coffee shop, and I'll finish out my degree someplace there, or take online classes or...or I don't know what. I'll commute. Come home on the weekends, drive up here for classes during the week, back down on Fridays. Take the job, baby!" Alex slid off the counter and into his arms. "*I'm* proud of *you*. This is way bigger than my promotion."

Nicholas smiled, but it dissolved into a frown. "Come on, Alex. Online courses? Is that even going to be the same? And commuting? You have a life here. *We* have a life here. Your education is the most important part of your life right now, aside from our marriage. You said that yourself."

"If you don't take the job because of me..." Alex pulled out the puppy dog eyes. "Seriously, Nicholas, I want this for you. This one's your dream."

"How did I get such a supportive man?" Nicholas cheesed, leaning in to kiss him, hands trailing down his back. He was tempted to stop making dinner and take Alex to the bedroom instead, show him how thankful he was to have his support. But Jade and Veronica would be waiting, so he held off, settling for another kiss.

"You were annoying as all get out until I couldn't resist you for another second."

"Right." Nicholas rolled his eyes and turned back to the food. He spooned the filling into the crust, his smile still plastered on his face. "Now I have to figure out how I'm going to tell Jade."

"That part, I can't help you with."

Chapter Twenty-Two

Speed Run

Nicholas leaned against Jade's kitchen counter, listening to the whirr of the blender as Veronica mixed up strawberry margaritas.

"So, I was telling her that no, me getting ordained does not mean I can marry her cats," Jade cackled.

Alex smiled. "Aw, why not? I bet your ordination carries down to animals too." He turned and tugged Nicholas's arm around his waist. "I mean, there's no reason not to take full advantage of your ability to marry people now that you've got the power."

"I told you, I'm exclusively using it for gay, loud weddings and not for animals or straight couples." Jade laughed again. Nicholas knew she was bluffing, that if any of her friends asked, she'd do it in a heartbeat, but he got it. There was very little worry for straight couples getting married... If they wanted to, they could throw a rock and find a church or a courthouse or a person in support of their wedding. Midwest weddings were a little trickier for couples like them.

"What if her cats are gay?" Nicholas asked.

"Then I'll consider it."

Nicholas hadn't said a word about the job offer yet. He knew as soon as he dropped that bombshell, the laughter would effectively be over. What was the right way to tell his friends he was planning on moving three hours away from them? What was the right way to explain that things would be different now? He was aware they all knew it was a possibility, that any of them could leave after school for the right job or the right path, but knowing they could end up apart and having it happen were two different things. And he hadn't told them he'd applied out of state, either, so it would blindside them far more than it did Alex.

So, he kept the conversation going. "I can see it now. Two little cats in their two tiny tuxedos, you standing there, joining them in matrimony..."

"I'd go to a wedding like that," Alex said.

Veronica shook her head. "No amount of allergy medicine in the world could get me in that building."

"That's V, single-handedly destroying lesbian stereotypes because of an allergy," Jade said. "We would have made such beautiful cat moms!"

"But we make great gecko moms instead," Veronica said, clutching her chest as if she was offended. Nicholas couldn't stop laughing.

As Nicholas laughed, his heart sank, jumbling his emotions. Moving away would mean less of this, fewer potluck dinners, no more laughter in Jade's kitchen, an end to the traditions they'd formed together. Three hours wasn't a huge distance, and if Alex chose to commute, he could always come back to visit, but popping over to say hello or have Jade swing by with a casserole wouldn't be happening anymore. The thought hurt.

"Margaritas are ready, and dinner is served!" Veronica called out, dishing the drink out into four different glasses, which she'd already rimmed with salt and colorful sugar, a lime wedge on each.

"Yeah, and since *you* made it, I won't taste the alcohol before any other flavor," Alex said, nudging Jade with a grin.

"That's it, pour it back in the blender, V, I need to add some more tequila just for Alex," she said, laughing and nudging him back as she headed for the table and sat in her regular seat for dinner parties, right next to Veronica.

Nicholas sat across from her and smiled. "I, for one, never know what to do with a cocktail with the right amount of alcohol. Jade and I have been friends for too long, I think." A lump rose in his throat. Standing in the kitchen, they'd already gorged themselves on chips and salsa and Veronica's raspberry black bean dip, but even if they hadn't, Nicholas feared his appetite would be gone. The thought of saying what he had to say was making him sick to his stomach. Still, he took a piece of the pollo magnifico, some recipe Jade had picked up from her family. "Thanks for dinner, guys."

"What're you being so sappy for?" Veronica asked. "There's no thanks necessary for a family potluck." And that's what they were, really. Family. They were chosen family, but they were family nonetheless, and Nicholas was struggling with the thought of leaving. He met Alex's eyes, giving him a sad smile. Alex looked better, smile lines back from how much he had been smiling in the past few days. Being at Jade and Veronica's only further lifted a weight off their shoulders. Nicholas knew his smile was rooted in multiple reasons, but a lot of his joy was due to these friendships, this loving part of their family that made him feel accepted. Alex had said as much again and again.

And Nicholas was tearing them apart. He took a small bite of the tortilla-wrapped chicken and cream cheese appetizer.

"Nicholas, don't tell me you're not hungry. We have your beef and potato taco pie to get through!" Veronica chastised. "Seriously, what's up?"

Nicholas swallowed heavily and looked at all of them. Now, he didn't have a choice but to say it. "I got offered a job today," he said quietly, because he wasn't sure how he felt about it now, the excitement from the phone call stripped as he considered the ramifications.

"Oh my God!" Veronica, of course, was instantly excited.

"I'm so proud of you," Jade blurted.

Nicholas's shoulders slumped, but he smiled. "Thanks, guys." He must have looked awful because Alex reached under the table and gave his hand a squeeze.

"Why are you not freaking out about this?" Veronica asked. "This is exciting! You should be all over the place, like, pulling a Tom Cruise and jumping on our couch or whatever!"

"I'm not sure I'm going to take it," he said, shrugging. "I mean, it's a great job. Genuinely my dream job. And I wanted it when I applied for it, thinking it would be perfect. I'd be doing exactly what I want to be doing." He was trying to justify this to himself, to find a reason to say yes when all he could do was think about how no, this wasn't the right choice. How could the job be the right choice if taking it led him away from this, the only family he had left aside from Alex?

"You say you're not going to take it and then you start going on about why you *should* be taking the job," Jade said. "What are you hung up on with it? Have you suddenly decided your dream job is absolute garbage?"

"No," Nicholas answered. "It's not that simple. I mean, on the exterior, it seems absolutely perfect. And they didn't hesitate to make the offer, so I can tell they genuinely want me. The issue is..." He sighed and took a sip of his margarita. "The issue is we'd have to move."

"You already moved once. Moving a little closer to work isn't that big of a deal. I mean, we've stayed friends with you moving a whole eight minutes away. It's not like you're not welcome in our apartment if you decide to take off for the other side of Omaha or something," Veronica said. And that was true, if he'd have taken any of the jobs he'd applied for on the other side of Omaha.

"God, Nicky, you're acting like you're going to be across the damn bridge!" Jade, ever helpful, was pointing out exactly why he couldn't do this, couldn't take the job. Had he gotten a job across the bridge, just over on the Iowa side of the border, it would have been nothing. They'd have been half an hour away, and there was no harm in that, but even then, Jade was acting like that was some kind of big difference.

"The job's in Kansas," Nicholas blurted, standing up to top off his drink, if only because he needed to walk for a moment, clear his head. "It's about three, four hours away."

"Oh." Jade suddenly appeared fascinated by her drink, picking salt off the rim and not making eye contact.

"I know. That's the problem. I'm not sure that moving right now is the right choice."

"When would you have to leave?" Veronica asked.

"In three weeks." Nicholas glanced at Alex. They had barely had time to discuss how quickly this would be happening.

"So, what about Alex's school?"

Alex glanced up from his food. "I'd be commuting, I think. Keeping the apartment here and coming up for class, then driving back down on weekends. Strategically timing it so I can skip a few classes and stay down a little longer, that kind of thing." He only had summer and fall left, pending a positive result with his thesis. They'd talked about it on the way over. With the right effort, he could be moved to Kansas by Christmas.

"And Nicholas would be coming up here sometimes too?" Jade asked.

"Yeah, I mean, we'd be keeping the apartment for him to go to school, so I'd imagine I'd be coming up here too," Nicholas said. He sat down again. "I'm torn. I mean, if I leave, then it means we'd all have limited time together."

Jade nodded. "I hate that, but I get it." Still, Nicholas could see the sadness in her eyes. He reached across the table and squeezed her hand.

"It doesn't change anything. We're family. We're just three-hours-apart family instead."

"I know."

Veronica furrowed her brow. "So, what about the wedding, then? Are you guys going to be planning that long-distance?"

Nicholas had been so wrapped up in the job and how it would affect Alex and his friends and their lives that he hadn't considered the piece of the puzzle that should have hit his mind first. "Oh my God," he said, turning to Alex. "I didn't even think about the wedding." Nicholas could almost feel the blood drain from his face.

"I'm sorry, hold up," Veronica said, holding a hand up. "*You* didn't think about the *wedding?*"

Nicholas shrugged. "I think I was just so wrapped up in the details of moving."

"Okay, V, pack up the food. I'm going to drive Nicholas to the hospital," Jade chuckled. Nicholas could see she was trying to force positivity but looking at her eyes revealed the truth. Her dam was moments from bursting, too, tears close to spilling over.

"I...I mean, I don't know what we'll do with the wedding."

Alex took his hand. "We'll figure it out."

For the rest of dinner, though, Nicholas couldn't keep his mind off it. "We'll figure it out" wasn't a satisfying answer because it meant having to think through the whens and hows. Would they plan through emails and on weekends? Could Alex juggle school with looking at venues? What if they planned a tasting with a bakery and Nicholas couldn't make it up to Omaha for the appointment because of a work snag? Should they call it off again, just until they got settled? When *was* the right time to have the perfect wedding?

"She brought a whole plate of cookies for the break room solely because she wanted to bake one night," Veronica said, midstory.

Nicholas realized he hadn't been paying attention, somehow lost in the middle of what they were saying. "Who?"

"The new girl at work, Alexandria," Veronica explained.

"Oh." Nicholas returned to his thoughts. He wasn't trying to be rude, but his mind couldn't keep up with the conversation as he considered the ramifications of moving *now*.

"I mean, they were almost the best cookies I'd ever had, besides those little Christmas bacon cookies that you make, Nic—"

"What if we got married now?" Nicholas blurted.

"What?" Jade asked.

"What if we got married now?" Nicholas repeated. He looked at Alex and then at Veronica. "Sorry. Didn't mean to interrupt, but..." He turned back to Alex. "What if we moved the wedding up?"

"Up to when? What?" Alex was clearly struggling to keep up by the way he glanced back and forth between everyone at the table. "I'm so confused."

"I mean I've been trying to think about how we would handle getting married—the venue, the tastings, the scheduling and planning and everything—if I was in Kansas and you were in Omaha. And I was thinking...what if we didn't?" He grabbed both of Alex's hands. "What if we got married before I move?"

"Okay, I'm not trying to be a downer here," Jade said, standing up from the table and carrying her plate to the sink, then bringing the chips and dip back with her. "But how the heck do you think you're going to get an entire wedding pulled together in three weeks? Especially, you know...*your* kind of wedding." He knew there was no shade meant by it, but even as he'd sent a few texts keeping her updated on the scale-down of the wedding, it wouldn't be a small feat to pull off.

"I don't know," Nicholas said. "But I really think we need to try." He turned to Alex. "Thoughts?"

"That's not a lot of time. Are you sure you *want* to speed it up?" Alex studied his face. "That's a lot of checklist items to skip or rush through."

Nicholas nodded. "You're sacrificing," he said. "You're uprooting again, moving to Kansas with me and commuting... I don't think it's a sacrifice for me to say that I really want to marry you, even if it means we go to the courthouse."

"Nicholas," Jade said, clearly confused by his sudden change of heart.

"We're *not* doing a courthouse wedding. You've got me too far into this wedding planning to cut it now. But I bet we could pull together a small event," Alex said. "If that's the plan, let's do it. Jade, you have time? Because the way I see it, as long as we have an officiant and two guys wanting to get married, we've got a wedding. Anything else we can get sorted is the icing on the cake."

"For you two? I always have time."

Chapter Twenty-Three

Mother, May I?

Alex scanned the list of details they hadn't taken care of yet. What had they been thinking, moving the wedding up so soon? Nicholas was working full time, almost to finals season, which meant stacks of papers and tests to grade. And Alex was working and going to school. All of that, while planning a wedding? They'd made a terrible choice. Still, he kept checking the checklist.

"Have you made your way through the guest list yet?"

"I've been working on it." Alex smiled, reaching for Nicholas's hand. "We got a handful of congratulations from people who couldn't come, two who said they'd send a gift as soon as we sent our new address, and my stepsister said they can't make it back from Thailand in time. My mother will be here."

"She okay with the changes?"

"She was pretty pissed. Not about the ticket prices for the trip, but...you know. I basically told her the wedding was happening now or it was happening later, and she could get on board or not get on board, but her support didn't change sh—"

"Wait, what?" Nicholas asked.

Alex's mother had been supportive when he'd come out to her. She acted like she'd known all along; that him being gay was no surprise. Of *course,* he was. But her tone had shifted when things got more serious with Nicholas, and they'd gotten worse after their engagement. He'd kept so much of that from Nicholas to avoid a fight, but now there was nothing to do but open up about it. "I started telling her about the date change, and she got huffy with me," he said. "I asked where that was coming from, and she said I was being selfish to change everyone's plans at the last minute for our new wedding. Even after I explained and said that we understood if people couldn't make it, she was still being a jerk."

Nicholas started to interject but closed his mouth again. Alex understood. What was anyone supposed to say to that?

"She kept pushing and pushing about how we needed to not rush into marriage just because you got a job, and maybe the time apart would be good for us to grow. She suggested if we took it slow, gave ourselves time apart...maybe we would change our mind." And that was the real issue. She'd been quietly kind and hopeful all along.

"So, she thinks we *will* change our minds."

"Yeah. If she goes along with our plans long enough, waits it out, we'll get to a point where we plan on not getting married. You should have heard her secret glee when we postponed. She tried to commiserate but—I don't know. Her tone of voice was all wrong for the situation." Tears welled up in Alex's eyes, and Nicholas moved to kneel in front of him on the bedroom floor.

"I'm sorry," he said. "Your mother's reaction isn't okay at all. It's not fair to you."

"I think, um." Alex sniffed. He couldn't get the words out without choking up. "I think even though they knew all along, or whatever, she thought I'd grow out of it. And now that I'm clearly not growing out of it, I think she thought maybe I'd at least not act on it." That was a lot of what he'd learned growing up. Being gay was a sin, but someone could choose not to act on that sin, marry a woman instead, or stay celibate forever. Alex wasn't like that. He wasn't okay with that. He was who he was, and he didn't want to apologize or hide it or feel ashamed of that anymore.

"Do you want to uninvite her?" Nicholas asked, taking his hand. "I'll follow your lead. If you don't want her here, we won't invite her."

"No, it's not... I don't know. She said before I marry someone, I should be certain they were who I wanted to spend my life with. I thought at first, she was just talking about her own insecurities. I mean, she's twice divorced, and that's not a big deal, but...I don't know. I ended up asking her if she would react like this if I was marrying a woman."

"And?"

"She burst into tears." There was no way to misread what she meant, no way to understand any other way. "What if she makes a scene at the wedding? I want her there, but...what if she ruins our wedding?"

"Have you seen V? The second she starts losing it, Veronica will have her butt out of there so fast she'll barely feel the door hit her after."

Alex nodded. "Are you going to be upset if I still invite her?"

"No," Nicholas said. "I would give anything to have my mother there on my wedding day. I'm not about to ask you not to have yours, supportive or not. If you want her there, the invitation is open to her. And if you don't, I support you in that too."

Alex smiled and leaned in to kiss him. "I'll ask V to be our bouncer and boot her if she starts a scene," he agreed.

"Perfect. And Alex? My mom would have absolutely loved you."

Alex wished he had gotten to experience that love personally because he needed it right now. Given what he knew about Nicholas's mother, though, he was taking that statement as gospel. Nicholas's mom *would* have loved him, and the knowledge helped ease his heart.

Chapter Twenty-Four

The Downside of Fast Decisions

A beautiful wedding. That was what Nicholas had dreamed of his entire life. A beautiful wedding with his family and friends there, with his beloved looking stunning. And that was the plan, a beautiful wedding. But at nine in the evening the night before the wedding, he was in full-on panic mode.

"Jade, can you run out and get some store-bought pie crusts?" he begged on the phone.

"Store-bought pie crusts?"

Nicholas could almost *hear* her eyebrow quirk up through the phone. "Jade, I'm desperate. Unless you can bring me some vodka, some Crisco, and about ten extra hours before the wedding, I'm not sure I can get it right."

"Vodka and Crisco sounds like a whole lot of cashier questions I don't want to contend with," Jade said. "It's like one of those games, the 'confuse your cashier in three items'."

"Jade, I'm serious!" Nicholas snapped, panicking. "Please. I'm begging you."

"I'll be over in half an hour with store-bought crust dough, vodka, and Crisco, because the second I show up with the dough, you're going to change your mind. Anything else I can get?" she asked.

"No. Just...thank you. Seriously. I know I'm losing my cool over this, but I don't know how else to handle our dessert getting so messed up." He sighed.

"You're allowed to be a little bit of a Groomzilla, Nicky. I'll be there soon."

Nicholas surveyed the damage after he hung up. Every single one of the crusts blackened, too dark to be edible. He didn't understand how they'd burned. He was good at baking, and pies were a dish he could make in his sleep. He'd reduced the cook time to account for the fact that the mini pies were single-serve, smaller than the others, but they still scorched. "*How*?" he lamented.

"Baby, it's fine," Alex said, walking in and giving him a kiss on the cheek. "No one is going to be as concerned about this as you are," he said softly. "We're going to have a beautiful wedding."

"Alex, the pies aren't a little overdone. They're burnt to a crisp!" They weren't burnt to a crisp, and Nicholas knew he was exaggerating a little bit, but they *weren't* edible.

"I think the oven runs hotter here," Alex said. "It's not your fault."

"They're still not up to my standards." He started to mix more filling, thankful he hadn't made all of the pies at once. Apple pies may have been out of the question—he'd burnt the apples too—but the other pies were possible, the peach-strawberry ones especially.

Nicholas surveyed the damage as he mixed the next batch of filling, shaking his head. Not good enough. None of what he'd made was good enough. But so long as the rest went off without a hitch, this would work. He pulled Alex in for a kiss. "Promise me that the rest is going to be fine," he lamented, voice tinged with frustration.

"Baby, as long as I'm marrying you, everything is great. Pies are just pies. You're doing a great job with them. Above and beyond."

Even with Alex's reassurance, Nicholas couldn't shake the nagging sense that things were going to go horribly wrong. Alex put on a movie, and Nicholas knew what he was doing. He was trying to coax him over to watch it and get his mind off their wedding. "Sweetheart," Nicholas reminded him. "There's no time. We get married tomorrow. I have to have the pies done tonight or we'll be up all night and I'll have bags under my eyes for the wedding photos." He was trying to stay as calm as he could. This was only the pies, he reminded himself. Jade was bringing more crust. Everything would be all right. He kept repeating that as he set the filling aside to coax the extra moisture out and discarded the parts of the previous pies he couldn't use. He picked at the pie crust, eating some. Yes, definitely overcooked. It no longer flaked, and it had that taste of burntness to it.

Jade didn't even knock when she got there. "Hey, here." She passed him the store-bought crusts. "I got these as fast as I could." Her hair was soaking wet, and she stood over the sink, wringing it out a little. "It's a downpour out there."

"No," Alex said.

"Yeah. It's raining cats and dogs and maybe a few sea lions, actually."

"No," Nicholas repeated Alex's sentiments.

"Guys, the barn is indoors. It's going to work out," Jade reassured them.

The weather forecast hadn't called for another round of rain, and Jade was right; they could just as easily move the outdoor parts of the wedding inside. The whole event would take some reimagining, but they could figure it out. Nicholas had seen the barn twice now, and he was sure they could sketch out a plan before they got there on how to tear down the wedding and set up the reception, holding both indoors if the rain didn't give. But the flooding, that was what concerned him. He scanned the kitchen cabinets and then started to take the items from the shopping bags Jade had carried in. There was no time to focus on the venue now. He turned his full attention back to the task at hand: new pies.

Chapter Twenty-Five

Flood Plain

Alex stared at the television screen and wondered at what point it would be safest to tell Nicholas what was happening. They'd called the venue the night before, confirming that the ground was a little marshy, but generally okay once everyone was inside. He and Nicholas had banked on the fact that it would be safe to use.

What no one had expected, apparently not even the venue owners, was for an upstream dam to burst and flood the entire plain below it.

Including the barn.

"Babe?" Alex called from the other room.

"What's up?" Nicholas looked downright dapper.

"I was heading out to pick up the tuxes and I turned on the news and—"

"No." Nicholas held his hands up. "Whatever you have to say, it better not be something about our wedding."

Alex moved, revealing the television behind him: the flooded plains, and the view from the helicopter flying over the area, the barn where their wedding was to be held coming into frame. At the same time, both of their phones vibrated with an apology text from the owner. "At least he's offering to refund the deposit," Alex said, reading it and sticking his phone back in his pocket. "He didn't have to do that." He felt sick for the families who lived in the flooded plain, who would be affected by the water, whether it ruined their homes or their crops or both. But he was also sick thinking about how the flood messed with their wedding.

"What good is it going to do? Our wedding is in nine hours and we don't even have a venue!" Nicholas yelped.

Alex hugged him. As far as he could tell, there was no easy solution to this. They'd barely managed to scrape together enough perfectly baked mini pies for the guests, and now they were battling against the weather. The rain continued to fall outside too. Changing venues wouldn't be easy, not on such short notice. "I don't know. I don't know what we're going to do, but I'm going to go pick up the tuxes, and you can go get the flowers. I'll meet you back here right after so we can load the car. We'll figure something out." Alex kissed his cheek.

On the drive to the bridal shop, he considered the possibilities. They had the option to postpone, but his mother had already flown in, and getting her here in the first place was enough of a feat. They could move the wedding to Kansas if they postponed further, maybe even move it back to the original date, but that inconvenienced more people. They could hold the wedding as planned, because everyone was there, but where would they have it? There wasn't exactly a perfect venue ready on a moment's notice. Or, they could elope, forget the wedding, and forget the problems, but somehow Alex didn't think Nicholas would go for that.

As he entered the tux shop, he willed there not to be any more issues. They couldn't handle another catastrophe, even if Nicholas was handling the first few better than Alex had anticipated. A small wedding was causing them both heart palpitations; Alex was thankful they'd downgraded from the overwhelming massive bash Nicholas had initially planned. The way this one was shaping up he wasn't sure they would have survived a larger wedding without a massive meltdown.

He wished they'd been able to pick up the tuxedos sooner, taken some of the pressure of the day off, but they hadn't been available on short notice until the day of. They'd have to work. "I'm here to pick up two tuxedos," he mentioned. "A white one with the mint vest and tie and a black one with the coral vest and tie."

Two tuxedos. Simple enough. After all, they weren't dealing with bridal gowns and massive amounts of alterations. These were rental tuxes, just right for them. Except when they brought out Nicholas's tux and showed it to him. "Those pants are the wrong size." He could tell before he even looked at the sizing. "That's a good six inches too short!" He glanced at the employee's face in desperation.

"This is the size we have on the form."

"No," Alex said. There was no way they had said the wrong size for the form. "Can you switch it out? Do you have another pair that he can swap to?" Even if they didn't carry his unusually tall size, any pants closer than these would work.

"It's prom season," the employee said. "To be honest, you're lucky we had tuxedos at all. We've called these in from other stores."

"So, call in longer pants from another store!" Alex insisted. "Please. I'm not trying to snap at you. It's just...our desserts got messed up and now our venue is flooded, the tux is the wrong size, and I'm not sure I can take another issue that takes away from my husband's perfect day." He was nearly in tears, feeling them sting at his eyes as his face crumpled. How the tables had turned; as much as he feared Nicholas being a Groomzilla on the day of the wedding, he was practically crying in a tux shop, strained and stressed. Maybe Nicholas was faring better.

"Listen, man. I'm sorry. I get it. I mean, when you're trying to book things out"—he squinted at the paper in front of him—"three weeks ahead of time, it seems like there's a high chance of running into issues like those."

Alex groaned. "I know! Okay, I know, we should have eloped, but my husband has dreamed of a big wedding his whole life and he leaves in three weeks and—why am I explaining this? Pants aren't going to magically appear if I justify our short-sighted planning to you." He tugged at his hair and glanced up at the guy. "Thank you. Seriously, these will work. I'll take them, and maybe he can find his own pants to work with it. I don't know." He shook his head.

"Listen, I'll give you a discount, okay? I'll knock some money off because I get that it sucks to have all this land on your big day."

"Thanks," Alex said. "That'll at least soften the blow when I take these home." He shook his head. "I don't know what I'll do if there's another problem today. I'm not sure how we'll handle it."

*

Nicholas paced in the middle of the flower shop. "So basically, you're saying you have...almost no flowers."

"I'm sorry, sir. We were already struggling with the floods impacting our stock of local flowers, and then the dam break cut off our shipment from out of town."

"And you don't keep any other cut flowers on hand?" He stared at the bare shelves, willing himself not to cry.

"We have some, but as we mentioned when you placed the short-notice order, we fill orders based on when we receive them in times where we've got limited stock. We had about fifty prom orders ahead of your wedding, and while we've been calling to try to get ahold of you, there isn't much we can do."

Nicholas hung his head. He understood they weren't to blame, and he understood that they did, in fact, warn him his short-notice wedding would be far down the list. He just hadn't anticipated such a limited supply.

"We had ordered the specific flowers you asked for, but again, the trucks are delayed from the floods. Normally it would be okay, and if you were flexible, we could fill with flowers we have, but..." She gestured at the same empty refrigerators and shelves Nicholas had been looking at. "I've got a few succulents left."

"Okay. We'll take your stock of succulents," Nicholas said, nodding. Cacti weren't exactly wedding plants, but they'd have to work.

"I'll add a list of other florists at the bottom who might have some flowers left. If you're able to drive across the bridge, there might be some florists in Council Bluffs who haven't been hit as badly with the flooding, but who knows what they'll have."

"Thank you," Nicholas said. At this point, he'd take what he could get.

Just as he was walking out of the door, a florist ran out with wildflowers in a vase. "Here. We had these sprouting out back, so they're freshly cut. It isn't much, but you might be able to pin them to your lapels."

"Thank you so much." Wildflowers, just like they'd wanted. These, of course, weren't wild grown like the others, but they were still the perfect aesthetic. He teared up. "How much do I owe you?"

"Just take them. And sir? Congratulations on your marriage."

Nicholas smiled and thanked her again. If they couldn't find anything else, at least they had wildflowers, a bright spot in their wedding scramble. Unfortunately, as he sat in his car and called through the list of other florists, including the ones across state lines, he was coming up empty-handed. The succulents and wildflowers were about all he could find. He dialed Alex's number, getting the voice mail instead of Alex himself. "Hey, sweetheart. Problem at the florist. They're tapped out on flowers and the flood means they're not getting any in right now. I've got a handful of succulents and a few other florists to drive through that have more succulents, some baby's breath, and a couple of potted orchids, but I'm not entirely sure what we're going to get in the end. I'll meet you at home. Love you."

Nicholas buried his head in his hands, elbows resting on the bottom of the steering wheel, and willed himself not to panic over this. "It's fine. Everything's fine." So long as there were no issues with the tuxedos, everything would be okay. He just couldn't believe they were this short on flowers, that all their plans were hanging by a thread. He glanced at the flowers in the passenger seat. *Yes. Everything will be okay.*

As he drove to the next florist, he thought about the worst-case scenarios. He'd mentally prepared himself for an aspect of their wedding to go wrong. *Of course.* They'd struggled with the fire, lost the binder and everything else, and they'd changed the wedding date, and they'd already called it off once. There was bound to be an issue or two; he'd talked himself through the possibility. But he hadn't banked on so much going wrong. He wasn't thinking of the bad in a way that stressed himself out; if he planned for the worst, anything better was an upgrade, not a let-down. It was the kind of tactic Alex would employ, and he wondered how he was doing, if he was doing any better with his half of the list. As he navigated the streets of Omaha, some of which were shut down due to the very same floods threatening to ruin his wedding, he told himself that no matter what happened, nothing would be as bad as the worst-case scenario.

He'd made the pies better, so despite only having one flavor instead of the assortment he'd hoped for, desserts were taken care of. Veronica had planned custom cocktails for the two of them—if nothing else to keep Jade from mixing them too strongly.

Mostly, the wedding was going to go well. He hoped. As long as the tuxes were fine, as long as he could find a few flowers to cobble together arrangements, they'd be okay. And then it hit him. They hadn't found a new venue. The wedding was in five hours, and everything else that had gone wrong had kept them from picking a new venue. He whipped his car into the parking lot and picked up his phone to call Jade.

"What's up, Nicky? Things okay?"

"No! We forgot to figure out a venue!" Nicholas yelped into the phone. How had he let it slip his mind? How had they not taken care of it the second they found out? His heart raced and his palms started to sweat. They were screwed. There was no way they could have a wedding now.

"Remember? I told you we were handling the venue, Nicholas. Last night, before I left, I said, 'don't stress about the venue,' and you agreed."

Nicholas had no recollection of the conversation, but if that was any indication of his mental state, it made sense that he'd have forgotten. "Right, so...what's the plan, then?"

"Seriously? I left you three voice messages about it," Jade lamented. "Okay, plan is, you come to my place. Do not even *think* about getting here before three. I've already texted everyone the new location, and I've already gotten the photographer on board. All you have to do is show up. Veronica's got the rest handled. How's the flower stuff going?"

"Awful," he vented. "In fact, I'm at the next florist now, so I have to go. Did you tell Alex where to go?"

"Unlike you, he answers his phone, so...yes. He'll meet you at the apartment as planned."

"Great. I'll see you then. And Jade? Thanks for everything." Nicholas couldn't help but smile. Every single plan they had was crumbling around them, but at least he had her, and Veronica, and their closest friends to help them out. He wasn't sure what he'd do without them.

*

Alex searched Nicholas's closet for any pair of nice slacks that would look remotely okay with the tuxedo he'd picked out. He found some that weren't perfect, but they'd work. He wished Nicholas would consider jeans. They could pull that off in a heartbeat. Jeans, the button-down shirts and vests, ditching the jackets altogether? It sounded a lot easier than trying to get slacks to work with the options they had.

He glanced at his watch. Four hours until the wedding and they hadn't finalized clothing, he had no idea what the flower situation was like, and he was glancing at his phone trying to cobble together a playlist for the reception between looking for something to wear. He wished he had some kind of playlist already planned, but before they'd changed wedding dates, Nicholas had been banking on hiring live music. That would have been remarkable, but now? It wasn't an option.

All he needed was a plan. A playlist, some clothing, and a plan. He just hoped Nicholas wouldn't be disappointed. As soon as he heard the door open, he rushed to the front door. "Okay, what's up?"

"We have a car full of baby's breath, about thirty succulents, some orchids, and a handful of assorted cut flowers that don't go together at all," Nicholas answered with a shrug. "Oh, and wildflowers. For our lapels. How are the tuxes?"

"Small hang-up. Your pants were way too short. I've been trying to find some that look okay, but so far it's all a nightmare."

Nicholas looked like he could cry. That was the last thing Alex needed, for Nicholas to lose it. He took both of Nicholas's hands, tugging him in and resting his forehead against his chest. "I'm sorry this isn't the wedding you dreamed of."

Nicholas's telltale sniffle said plenty. "It's a wedding. I'm marrying you. I'm happy."

Alex knew him better than this, knew the tone in his voice, knew the way that he was trying to resist showing how upset he really was. "I'm happy to be marrying you," Alex told him. "We'll figure it out. Maybe we can have a vow renewal next year, with a proper wedding, the one you really want, and it'll be perfect."

Nicholas nodded. "It's perfect. It is."

Alex tried to believe him, or at least believe he really felt that way. "Let's look at this clothes situation." Nicholas tugged his hand and Alex followed.

"I've been trying to get a wedding playlist together. I should have thought of it sooner, but for some reason it hit me at the last seco—"

"Oh!" Nicholas exclaimed. "I have one. I have a playlist." He pulled his phone from his pocket and passed it to Alex. "Look."

Alex sank down on the edge of the bed and scrolled through. Hundreds of songs from the time they'd been together, page after page of songs reflecting their relationship, from the cheesy to the beautiful, the slow to the manic, the silly to the sentimental. "Oh my gosh," he whispered.

"I had been putting it together for a long time, but I didn't realize it would come in handy now," Nicholas said, sitting on the bed beside him and rubbing his back. "I assumed it would be something fun for us to look back on. I didn't think it would end up being our wedding playlist."

Glancing at him with tears in his eyes, Alex smiled. "You single-handedly saved our reception, I think." Of all the parts of their wedding going wrong, this was a sign that things would be okay. Alex clung to that hope.

Chapter Twenty-Six

Don't Hold Your Breath

Back when Nicholas had planned for them to have different outfits entirely, he'd dreamed of a first look moment, a big reveal of the outfits they were each wearing in a private ceremony captured by the photographer. The day didn't allow for that, not with the schedule, the delays from the weather, and all the changes. And Nicholas worried he'd be upset missing out on that moment, but now, as Nicholas squeezed Alex's hand, he realized he didn't. They were both dressed in well-fitting slacks and white button-down shirts, with their respective colorful vests and ties. Why have a first look? They were basically wearing the same thing. A first look might have made sense had they chosen large gowns, or even drastically different suits, but they hadn't. They looked so similar today, so perfectly matched to each other. And the mint set off Alex's red hair beautifully. He wouldn't have wanted to delay seeing him for a single second.

Now that they were dressed, everything else was out of their hands. They couldn't change the wedding, couldn't finalize anything. The ceremony was set in stone.

So, they drove to Jade's without making a production of getting dressed. He just hoped that she was right, that the decor was handled. As he held Alex's hand, he walked up the stairs to her apartment. "Okay. We're here," he said.

"Good, because so is everyone else," she said, swinging the door open. He smiled, giving her a hug. "You guys ready for the best freaking wedding on the planet?"

Nicholas snorted. He wasn't entirely sure they could classify this garbage show of a wedding so far as the best ever, but whatever. He was willing to try. "Sure," he said, smiling. There was no point worrying or getting worked up about what he couldn't control. He kept telling himself that. *It's out of your hands. The wedding is done. For all intents and purposes, all you can do now is say "I do" and call it good.* Still, his heart raced, and he wasn't sure if he was having palpitations because he was getting ready to get married, or because this was about as far from the wedding of his dreams as he could get.

He hoped it was the former.

"Okay. You're going to go get pictures done, and then you'll walk back up here, and we'll head to the wedding location together for the rest of the pictures and the ceremony," Jade said, putting a hand on each of their backs. "Go on. Trust us. Leave your keys and we'll unload your cars."

Nicholas nodded. Everything really *was* out of his hands now.

*

Panic. Outside of all the love he held for Alex, and the fact that they were getting married, Nicholas felt *panic.* Alex held his hand and squeezed it, and Nicholas squeezed back. He wished he could see something. Anything, really. Instead, his eyes were completely closed. Jade had insisted on blindfolding them. He'd hated the idea, but she'd gone to so much trouble for them, and he wasn't about to protest now. So, he let her blindfold him. He tried to resist the urge to cry when she'd told him that she knew this wasn't his dream venue, that the wedding wasn't going as planned, and he'd nodded and forced a smile. There was no going back. For all the ways he hyped himself up in the car, knowing whatever happened ended with an upgrade—a wedding and a husband—his heart still hammered in his chest.

The second they'd gotten to Jade's, she'd asked for the keys and told him to go get pictures with their photographer, that she'd handle everything. She'd done a wonderful job with the engagement party, but Nicholas had hesitated. This was his wedding, and he worried he was letting himself down if he didn't have his hands in it. There was no time to argue, though, not when his friends were offering the help they desperately needed, and not when the photographer was ready for them. So, he'd followed Alex to the photographer, gotten photos together, and now, there was no putting it off. He was about to see where he'd be getting married, without any idea what he was going to see when he opened his eyes.

He wasn't mourning the wedding he'd spent so many years planning. Not anymore. But in some ways instead, he mourned the wedding he pictured them having before his job and life threw a wrench into their plans, before flooding and last-minute issues had messed it all up. He'd read an article about a bride who had her wedding in the middle of a blackout in New York City, and the pictures had turned out beautifully, but somehow, he couldn't picture his own wedding overcoming all the obstacles. Still, in his own heart, he knew what mattered.

His mother was here, in his heart. His father, his grandmother, his aunt: they'd all be proud. Jade and Veronica were there. Brandon and Olivia were there. All their closest friends were. And Alex's mother, which by extension, was his family now too.

Most importantly, Alex was there. Alex was there and ready to marry him—Alex, who looked absolutely gorgeous. As the sun was on the very fringes of setting around them, the warmth of the rays settled on his skin. He let Jade guide him down the hill and, hand in Alex's, he felt peace. Whatever happened now, happened. As panicked as he was, as much as this wasn't the wedding he'd anticipated, he was going to marry Alex. And that was really what mattered to him.

"Are you ready?" Jade asked.

"As ready as I'll ever be," Nicholas said. He braced himself for the absolute worst: for the succulents to look out of place and the colors to be messed up and the entire setup to be absolutely ruined. Instead, as her fingers untied the knot carefully, his heart raced. Anything could be on the other side of the blindfold, so he took a deep breath, and as she moved the cloth, he kept his breath held.

"Nicholas?" Jade asked.

"Yes?"

"You can open your eyes now," she laughed.

Nicholas hadn't realized how much he was hesitating, that he'd closed his eyes as she took the blindfold off. He opened his eyes. "Oh my God."

Alex said the same in unison, both of them scanning the scene in front of them. As the sky started to light up with pinks, it illuminated an arch of balloons in their colors, a long burlap runner across the ground, with mismatched chairs on each side for their family and friends. Nicholas held Alex's hand and stepped forward, eyeing Brandon in the front. "I hope you don't mind my guitar. We weren't sure how to get the speakers loud enough."

"It's perfect," Nicholas said. The front had two benches, lined with succulents and candles, a music stand wrapped in twinkle lights. Sure, most of the wedding was improvised, but it was beautiful. "You guys did all of this?" he asked.

"Veronica's been out here working on this while we were working on blowing up balloons for the arch and setting up the reception space... You'll see it after." So, the surprises weren't over. That was okay, Nicholas assumed. If the reception space was anything like this, it would be a dream too. He smiled and leaned in, hugging Jade and then Veronica, watching as their guests sat. At the front, he saw four chairs with four picture frames. From here, he couldn't see the frames, but he knew what was in them by instinct. Alex had asked about photographs of his parents weeks before, and he knew his closest family members were here in spirit, occupying the seats they would have held for his big day. "How about we do this before the sun's gone?" Jade asked.

Nicholas nodded. For all the anxiety he'd had about this wedding from the start, nothing could have prepared himself for the perfection now. In the rare stretch where it hadn't been raining, they were getting married, on the hill by the side of their old apartment building overlooking the flooded plain, the sunlight glistening across the water that stood there. He squeezed Alex's hand, and as they walked down the aisle, Brandon started to play a soft acoustic melody Nicholas couldn't place, but that suited the moment all the same. Jade made her way to the music stand before them, smiling, and Nicholas could hear the click of the camera as it captured the dying daylight that guided them into their new life together.

He glanced over at the photographs, squeezing Alex's hand again. "Thank you for helping me honor them," he said softly.

But then Alex nodded and took a detour, walking toward the photographs and crouching down near them, careful not to kneel and get his knees dirty. "Thank you," he whispered, running his hand down the frame holding Nicholas's mother's picture. "I wish I could tell you in person."

Nicholas teared up, leaning down beside him. "Thanks, Ma," he said softly. "I would have never been open to love if it weren't for what you and Dad showed me." He glanced over at his father's photograph and then at Alex. "Ready?"

"Heck yes, I'm ready."

Chapter Twenty-Seven

This Vow

Alex couldn't keep himself from crying. Not as Nicholas stood there, holding his hands, facing him. He pulled out a piece of paper from his pocket, looking into Nicholas's eyes.

"Nicholas, the first memory I have of you is standing in a grocery store, hearing you before I could even see you, your voice booming along to piped-in Christmas music. That's sort of how it is now; I hear you every morning before I see you, as you do the loving things that make my life so special. With every breakfast in bed, every late-night talk, and every blanket fort we build together to recapture the magic of those first days together, I fall more and more in love with you.

"You helped me become myself. You helped me find the parts of me that I wouldn't unlock for anyone, and you helped me open my heart. That is what I treasure about you, the way you make me more comfortable with who I am. But I also treasure that you give me all there is to give of yourself. You forgive me for my mistakes. You tend to me when I'm sick, and you take it in stride when I can't return the favor without risking burning down an entire apartment.

"I always thought that when I found the person I'd marry, I'd be standing there, knowing I had met my equal. But Nicholas, I haven't. I haven't even come close. Because we're not equal. You far outshine me in so many ways, making me want to do better for myself and for you. And the part I can't get past is how you look at me and tell me what I'm saying isn't true. I can see it in your eyes now, and I knew it was coming, which is why I was able to write it down in these vows. You tell me that you don't outshine me, that we are equal, and that's the beauty in our relationship. We're not, because we're so, so different. But none of that matters, because for all of my flaws, you have a strength, and for all of my strengths, you have those little imperfections that make me love you more.

"I can't imagine life without you in it, and I cannot imagine today without you here in front of me. Nicholas, I love you. And I'm excited for wherever life takes us, to Kansas, and to wherever else we go after. Our adventure is just beginning, and I'm really thankful for you."

Alex reached up and wiped the tears from his own eyes and then wiped the tears that were running down Nicholas's cheeks. He hadn't intended to make them both cry but he couldn't help it. He meant every word he had said, meant the ways that he loved Nicholas beyond all measure and comparison.

Perhaps he should have been prepared for the fact that Nicholas's vows would be equally emotional, but he couldn't. He couldn't think ahead to the ways those would bring him to tears or he would have never gotten through his own.

"Alex," Nicholas said, his own paper in hand. Alex could tell his hand was shaking by the way the paper trembled. But then Nicholas put the paper away, folding it carefully and slipping it in his pocket again. "Alex. You've given me so much joy. As I look at you and listen to you, all I can think about is how happy you make me. You make me happy to the point that I'm crying too hard to read the vows I wrote, so you're going to have to deal with that and read them later." He leaned in and kissed Alex's cheek, holding his hands again. "You say we aren't equals. Maybe you're right about that. Maybe you're right that we are too different in so many ways, but all I can think about is how hard you try. Within days of moving in, you'd cleaned out my shower knowing that would make my life easier, but that I'd never make time to do it. You painstakingly scanned my family recipes knowing that I'd be devastated if I lost them, but that I'd never take the time to scan them in myself, and that came in handy. You worked tirelessly to go to a cooking class and learn how to confidently make soups that would make me feel better to prevent ever having another kitchen fire like the one we had again.

"Alex, you go above and beyond to show me love in every possible way. You presume that we could never love each other equally because you don't love me the way I love you, because you love me in your own, different, perfect Alex way. And the thing is, that's why I love you. If I found someone who loved me the way I loved, I'd be bored to tears.

"You make my life more interesting. I've never met a man who could belt every single song in Guns N' Roses's catalog, while appreciating the fact that I'm more into Ariana Grande than classic rock. But I've also never met anyone willing to pull all the couch cushions down and tack sheets to the walls to make the most brilliant blanket fort I've ever seen.

"Alex, you give me so much hope and so many dreams for the life we'll have. Our kids are going to think you're fascinating as you tell them stories about how we met, and the adventures we have to this day. Things as simple as going for coffee in the mornings become an adventure with you, turning into all-day dates that end in coffee the next morning too. Before I met you, I was singing alone in my kitchen, begging my friends to come make sweets with me—Jade probably still has the text receipts to prove it—and now I've got you. A built-in best friend who keeps me sane and happy. I don't know what I'd do without you by my side every single day, and I know I've said that, but I can't help saying it again. Alex, you make my life more comfortable, more happy, and you make me fall in love with you every single day. I love you, and I cannot wait to make this an official lifelong arrangement, because you're stuck with me now."

Alex had tears running down his face and was thankful he'd foregone the concealer he'd considered wearing to hide a few bits of nervous acne that had cropped up. He had a feeling his makeup would be destroyed had he worn it with the way Nicholas's words got to him.

Even as they did more traditional vows following their personal messages to each other, he struggled to keep his composure. Right now, he was committing to the man he loved, to a lifetime with him, and that affected him in ways he couldn't fully express.

"I love you," he mouthed at Nicholas not long before the end of the ceremony.

"I love you too," Nicholas answered, mouthing the words back to him.

Alex stayed looking at Nicholas, eyes trained on him, until Jade asked if they had the rings. He smiled at her, reached in his pocket, and his heart sank. "Did you pick up the rings from the jewel—"

"No. Oh no, you didn't?" Nicholas asked.

Alex shook his head. "I... It slipped my mind with the flood and the...the tuxedos and..."

"I totally forgot too. I had the checklist on the fridge and... Crap!"

Alex studied his face and started to laugh. "I wonder if anyone's ever said 'crap' in the middle of their own wedding before," he mused.

"Probably not at a wedding they actually decided to still have," Nicholas said. He had tears in his eyes as he started to laugh, too, and Alex figured it was probably because crying harder wouldn't have done any good. He took Nicholas's hands and looked him in the eyes, pulling him in and hugging him.

"I don't need rings to marry you," Alex said in his ear, rubbing his back through his vest. "Let's do this and get them later." Nicholas nodded, pulling back.

"Jade, we're doing it live!" he joked. There was no changing it now.

She smiled. "Okay. Skipping the rings part. In that case, it looks like you two are now officially husband and husband. You may now kiss your husband."

Alex didn't wait. With no hesitation, he leaned in and placed his hand on Nicholas's cheek, kissing him softly just as the sun started to finally dip below the horizon. "I love you," he said again as he pulled back.

"I love you too," Nicholas answered him.

They were married. They were actually, against all the odds and every possible obstacle, married.

And Nicholas was smiling like he'd won the lottery.

*

Had anyone told Nicholas that his wedding would go the way it had, he might have clutched his wedding binder to his chest and laughed in their face, saying, "No, I've got a plan. It'll *never* go that wrong." No one ever planned for the worst-case scenario for real. He looked at Alex, his *husband,* from across the room. They were in the community room of their old apartment building, but Brandon and Olivia had worked with Veronica to transform it the night before, as soon as they found out the venue wasn't going to work out. The ceilings were draped with twinkle lights, just like the ones in their many, many blanket forts. As he caught Alex's eye, all he could think of was how much he loved him.

His wedding didn't need to go right. Not really. His wedding could be an absolute insane mess—as it had been—and it wouldn't have changed the way he felt about Alex. So, as he looked at him in the complete opposite of the dream reception location he'd imagined, there was no pang of regret or worry or sadness that it hadn't been the reception he'd dreamed of. The warmth in his chest and the glow of the lights against Alex's face said everything he needed it to.

This was the way their reception was always supposed to go, he imagined. He looked at Jade, serving up mini pies to guests who sat around the tables they'd set up, having forgone the actual dinner service for desserts and snacks. Who needed a chicken dinner when there were lemon white chocolate cookie bars available, or his mother's strawberry pretzel dessert?

Alex's mother was here. And so far, she hadn't said a word at all. No words were better than negative words though. She was here. That was support enough. True acceptance could come later.

Everything felt right in this moment. His love, his husband, was right there. And he was happy. As he poured himself a cupful of the punch that had been deemed "Holiday Honey," a nod to the time they met, he smiled. The drink was one of two signature cocktails that night. The other—"Ceremony at Sunset"—was delicious, but this was sweet and strong, much like Alex. He sidled over to him with an extra glass. "Hey, husband."

"Hey," Alex said, kissing his cheek.

"So. We're married now."

"Actually, officially married," Alex said. "Does it count before we have rings?" he joked, elbowing Nicholas in the side.

"Oh, probably not, you know? We're probably complete and total frauds. You know, maybe this is why they say we're upending traditional marriage and ruining everything. We can't even have a traditional ceremony without messing it up!" Now, the mountains of mess-ups were funny. When they looked back at the pictures from their wedding day, they'd be able to tell their kids that they had so much love in their lives, they didn't need a perfect wedding. The right amount of love could make up for anything.

Nicholas turned and set his cup down, tucking Alex's hair back into place, and he kissed him, plush lips meeting gently as they focused on each other, the sole center of a busy room of people there to celebrate them. For a moment, the music seemed to stop. Or perhaps it actually did, the speaker cutting out as the Wi-Fi went down...again. Perfect? It didn't exist. Except maybe in each other.

Chapter Twenty-Eight

Honeymooners

Nicholas kissed his way down Alex's body, and Alex's fingers tangled in his now-messy locks. Their wedding night wasn't the dream, lavish honeymoon Nicholas had expected to have, with too much packing to be done for them to actually go anywhere to celebrate, but what better way to celebrate than spending the night tangled up in each other?

Alex had told him that, moments before. "I'm glad we didn't pay for a hotel. We wouldn't have made it out of bed anyway." The words echoed in Nicholas's head now as he rubbed a slick finger along Alex's entrance, teasing him before pressing inside, lips wrapped around his length. Alex was right. There was no point in going anywhere because this is all they'd planned to do with their night after their wedding. This, and talk about the future. They'd been discussing the future since they'd been together, after all, and they'd been intimate like this for quite some time. But somehow, Nicholas knew this *felt* different with the weight of their wedded bliss on them now. If the sounds Nicholas was eliciting were any indication, Alex was in agreement, enjoying it thoroughly.

Alex arched up off the surface of the bed, and Nicholas knew he was doing something right, so he did it again. "Oh, God, Nicholas...if you're wanting to...oh..." Nicholas smiled around him. *If you're wanting to get inside me, you better do it, because I won't last like this.* Alex didn't need to finish his sentence. Nicholas knew. Perhaps it was telepathy, or maybe they simply knew each other in intimate ways he couldn't explain. Either way, he smiled wider.

"Okay," he said, words more breath than sound as he kissed his way back up Alex's body, lingering at the parts that gave Alex the most pleasure, sucking at his ribcage and working his lips to Alex's nipples, flicking his tongue over one as his fingers explored the other. "Okay." He kissed Alex deeply. "My *husband,*" he whispered.

"Your husband," Alex answered before kissing him again. Nicholas lifted Alex's leg over his shoulder, watching as he pushed inside. This never got old, and he imagined given enough time, it never would.

"I love you, Alex," he breathed.

"I love you."

And Alex did love him. In words and vows and moments together through the past year and four months, Alex had loved him. And in every moment now, with every gasp and moan and arch of his back, Alex loved him. They were meant to be, just like this, entangled like this. Alex quivered beneath him, their lips locking, the sweat of their passion between them, glistening in Nicholas's chest hairs as he licked along Alex's jaw, teasing his earlobe with his tongue.

"Oh!" Alex moaned, tensing beneath him.

"Does it feel different now that we're married?" Nicholas teased. Alex rarely finished so soon, but he was close. That much was evident on his face.

"No...yes...better," he moaned. Nicholas smiled. Exactly as Alex said, this did and didn't feel different now they were married. This was as beautiful as their passion had ever been, but with their life ahead holding bright for the future. "I love you!" he repeated.

"I love you," Nicholas said back to him, an echo of his words and his breath and his kiss. Nicholas worked deeper into him, hitting the places that made Alex come unglued, and Alex gripped the sheets, tightening around Nicholas and pulling him closer to the precipice along with him. "I'm close," he moaned, and Alex nodded, resting his head against Nicholas's chest, watching the last few pushes before they were both collapsing in a heap on each other, breathing heavy and hard and ragged.

"Wow," Nicholas said between gasped breaths.

"Wow," Alex echoed back to him.

His phone buzzed on the bedside table. "Ignore it," Nicholas mumbled. They'd deal with it in the morning.

Alex nodded. "You know, I could go for some of that sponge cake."

Nicholas laughed. "Yeah? Grab a blanket. Let's go." He was already pulling off Alex and heading for the kitchen, skin bare as he heard Alex padding behind him, wrapped in a comforter.

*

Alex rolled over. "Who the hell is calling this early on our *honeymoon?*" he grumbled.

"Someone who doesn't know we're on our honeymoon?" Nicholas asked, peeking one eye open and trying to spare himself the bright morning light. "Probably a scammer. Just ignore—"

Too late. "Hello?" Nicholas waited for the inevitable grumbling, but none came. "Are you serious?" Alex's eyes met Nicholas's. "Yeah, I'll...I'll let him know." He paused. Nicholas strained, but he couldn't hear the words on the other end. "Thank you so much. I'll give you a call back as soon as I can."

"What was that?" Nicholas asked, sitting up, clutching the warm covers to his body. He rubbed his eyes, the boxes they'd already packed for their move coming into view.

"That was our old landlord," Alex said.

"What?"

"They haven't finished renovations on our old apartment, but they have a unit opening up in two weeks. They'd be willing to let us stay there and then transfer to our old apartment as soon as it's done."

That was tempting. The place where they'd started their story, renewed and renovated, ready for them to live there again. They could go back to the lives they had, let Alex finish his school in Omaha, keep them in one place for longer. They'd be surrounded by their friends and their chosen family here, the life they had built together, the life Nicholas had started building before Alex came into the picture.

The offer was everything he had ever hoped it would be. The chance for life to return to normal teased at the forefront of his brain. Before he could say "yes," and tell Alex he'd do it in a heartbeat, Alex shook his head.

"We should go."

"Are you sure?" Nicholas asked him. In part, he'd thought Alex would be more opposed to moving than he would. He'd just moved to Omaha from LA, finally gotten settled here, and now Nicholas was asking him to uproot. Alex didn't even have a reason to move, Nicholas aside. He could be happy here. He already had his job, his life, his school.

"I'm sure. This could be a really amazing start for us," Alex said, reaching for his hand and squeezing it. "What do you think?"

"I think staying would be easier," Nicholas admitted. "I mean, think about it. We've already mostly packed, so all we'd have to do is take our stuff across town. We'd have everyone here to help us unload. You could keep your job and keep going to school here. We wouldn't have to do any of the back-and-forth stuff." Alex had already applied to a school in Kansas, closer to Nicholas's new job. But he hadn't heard back. As things stood now, he'd be staying in this apartment and commuting back and forth on the weekends. Nicholas hated to disrupt his life so substantially.

"When the heck have we ever done things the easy way?" Alex asked him.

"That's true," Nicholas said. "You could get the apartment, stay there while you commute... We could ditch this place."

"Why?"

"I mean, you liked being there better," Nicholas said.

"Yeah, I liked it because that was home. Because you were there. Jade and Veronica aren't that far away. And besides, there's a bathtub here," he teased. "Nicholas, you made that place home. You made it safe. You made it comfortable. No point in working on this lease and then on that lease or whatever. Let's just...go. Like we planned."

"So, we're moving to Kansas, huh?"

"We're moving to Kansas."

"And we're saying goodbye to our old apartment?"

"We already did," Alex reminded him.

"Right. And we're saying goodbye to Jade and Brandon and Veronica and Olivia and everyone else here?"

"They're only three hours away. And you're going to have to come visit me sometimes. I'm not just driving back and forth by myself," Alex reminded him, giving him a quick peck on the cheek.

"That's true. So...a new adventure, huh?"

"Everything always is with you."

*

Nicholas stood at the back of the U-Haul, tears in his eyes as Jade stepped out of it, arms emptied of the last box. "No moving binder?" she asked.

"No moving binder," Nicholas said. "Don't need it. I let go of micromanaging situations, right?" He chuckled, knowing he couldn't let go of it forever. He reached for her, tugging her in for a tight hug.

"I can't believe you're leaving me," she said, voice full of choked-up emotion.

"I can't believe it either."

"You really can't stay?"

"I'm afraid not," Nicholas said. "You'll watch the apartment for us?"

"Nah. I'm going to let it get overrun by squatters. Maybe unleash some rats in there. Let a hard freeze come in and bust all the pipes. I think that's good payback for leaving me stranded in Omaha," Jade said, laughing.

"How rude," Nicholas answered, elbowing her.

"I'll watch it. And Alex will be back next month?"

Nicholas nodded. That was the plan. Alex would follow him down to Kansas City, spend a month getting their new home ready, and then he'd make the drive back up, splitting his time between the two places as he got his degree. Eventually, they'd be in one city. Eventually, they'd have one home to their name. Until then, Nicholas could pretend that this wasn't goodbye forever. After all, it wasn't. He still had years ahead with Jade by his side. Or, at the other end of the telephone, three hours apart. "You're coming down for Thanksgiving," he reminded her.

"Shut the heck up. Don't even talk to me about Thanksgiving," she chastised. "Talking about Thanksgiving makes it seem like you're not coming back before then."

She was right. They'd specifically decided against talking too much about the distant future and focus on the right-away stuff. "Okay. I'll see you next month, and I'll call you when we get to Kansas," Nicholas promised, giving her another tight hug. He'd already told Veronica goodbye before she headed to work, and already bid Brandon and Olivia farewell at a dinner party the night before.

Jade was the last goodbye he had in Omaha. And far more than the apartment or his plans for his wedding and anything else he'd said goodbye to, she was naturally the hardest goodbye to say. He hugged her again. "Bye, Jade. See you next month."

"Bye, Nick. Mail me some chocolate chip cookies when you start testing out that new oven of yours."

"You got it."

Nicholas turned back to Alex, watching as he closed the U-Haul and hugged Jade.

"You ready?" he asked Nicholas.

"As ready as I am for everything else," Nicholas said. "Yeah. I'm ready."

He climbed into the passenger seat as Alex started their trip playlist, the first few notes of one of Nicholas's favorite pop songs trickling through the air. Nicholas turned it up, leaned back in the seat, and smiled, belting the lyrics. He didn't miss the loving look on Alex's face as Alex glanced at him before shifting into drive.

"Hey, Alex?"

"Yeah?"

"How long do you think it'll be before I earn some paid vacation? I think after all this, we deserve a real honeymoon."

Nicholas's Springtime Recipes

Homemade Toaster Pastries

2 pie crusts (homemade or store bought)

Jam or jelly for fruit flavored toaster pastries (see below)

Fresh or frozen fruit for fruit flavored toaster pastries (see below)

Brown sugar, butter, and cinnamon for brown sugar flavored toaster pastries (see below)

½ c. powdered sugar

1 tbsp. milk

Sprinkles, if desired

Cut pie crusts into 16 equally sized rectangles.

Fill 8 rectangles with filling (approximately ½ tbsp. jam and pieces of fresh fruit for fruit-flavored pastries; 1 tbsp. brown sugar plus 1 tbsp. butter and 1 tsp. cinnamon for brown sugar cinnamon pastries).

Top each filled crust with a plain crust, sealing sides well.

Bake at 425 degrees for 10-11 minutes, until pastries are golden brown.

Mix powdered sugar with milk, adding milk 1 tsp at a time until desired consistency is reached.

Glaze toaster pastries and top with sprinkles if desired.

Let cool 5-10 minutes before eating, or seal in an airtight container

NOTE: filling may be hot after baking. Enjoy within two days. Do not warm in pop-up toasters.

Makes 8 pastries.

Mama's Travelers Sticky Biscuit Cake

For biscuit dough
2 c. sifted flour
½ tsp. cream of tartar
2 tbsp. sugar
½ tsp. salt
4 tsp. baking powder
½ c. shortening
⅔ c. cold milk
1 egg, slightly beaten

For cake
Biscuit dough (see above)
¼ c. melted butter
2 c. brown sugar
1 c. chopped nuts
1 c. raisins
Generous sprinkle cinnamon

In large bowl, sift together flour, cream of tartar, sugar, salt, and baking powder.

Cut in shortening until mixture resembles corn meal.

Gradually add milk, then add egg and mix well.

Knead exactly five times on a floured surface, then roll to ¼ inch thickness.

Brush with melted butter to the edges.

Sprinkle heavily with brown sugar, raisins, nuts, and cinnamon.

Roll up into jelly-roll style log.

Slice into 1½ inch thick slices, then lay flat in heavily buttered 9-inch by 9-inch pan.

Sprinkle with any filling that fell out during the cutting process.

Bake at 350 degrees for 30-40 minutes until golden and bubbly.

Serves 9.

Blueberry Peach Coffee Cake

1 box blueberry muffin mix, plus ingredients listed on box

1 can diced peaches

¼ c. sugar

¼ c. flour

½ tsp. cinnamon

2 tbsp. butter

Rinse and drain blueberries from muffin mix. Drain peaches. Place peaches and blueberries on paper towels to dry and set aside.

To make crumble topping, mix sugar, flour, and cinnamon in a small bowl. Cut in butter until crumbly.

Prepare muffin mix according to package directions, omitting the blueberries. Pour muffin batter into greased 9-inch by 9-inch pan.

Place peaches on top of batter, then evenly sprinkle with blueberries. Top with crumble topping.

Bake coffee cake at 400 degrees for 25-27 minutes.

Let cool for 15 minutes before cutting into squares and serving.

NOTE: this recipe requires a muffin mix where the blueberries are in a separate can, not mixed within the powdered mix.

Serves 9.

Chicken and Dumplings

Whole chicken (or equivalent 4-5 lbs. weight in chicken breasts or thighs)

1 stick butter

10-12 c. water

Medium onion, diced

3 tbsp. minced garlic

3 bay leaves

Salt and pepper to taste, additional seasonings as desired

6 c. flour, plus more for rolling

3 tsp. baking powder

2 tsp. salt

1 c. vegetable oil

1½ c. chicken broth (from pot)

4 eggs, beaten

Place chicken in large pot with water, butter, onion, salt and pepper to taste, garlic, seasonings, and bay leaves. Simmer until chicken is thoroughly cooked.

Remove chicken from broth, deboning and tearing chicken into small pieces, placing chicken back in broth.

Bring broth to a boil while preparing the dumplings.

For dumplings:

Mix flour, baking powder, 2 tsp. salt, 1½ c. broth from pot, vegetable oil, and eggs until a dough forms.

Roll out pieces of dough and cut into squares approximately 1½ square inches in size.

Place dough pieces into boiling broth, stirring occasionally until dough is cooked.

Serve hot and garnish with parsley or green onions if desired.

Overnight French Toast Casserole

1 loaf French bread, diced

1 can diced peaches, drained

6 eggs

1 c. half and half

1 c. milk

½ tsp. plus 1 tsp. cinnamon, divided

1 tsp. salt

1 tsp. vanilla extract

½ stick salted butter, softened

¼ c. brown sugar

Tear or dice French bread into bite size pieces and place in the bottom of a slow cooker.

Mix diced peaches with French bread.

In separate bowl, combine eggs, half and half, milk, sugar, salt, vanilla, and ½ tsp. cinnamon.

Pour egg mixture over bread mixture and allow to soak for at least one hour.

Combine butter, brown sugar, and remaining cinnamon. Fold into bread mixture.

Cook on warm for 8 hours or overnight, on low for 4 hours, or on high for 2 hours.

Serves 6.

Blueberry Yogurt Bars

1½ c. instant oats

1 c. flour

1 c. brown sugar, packed

½ tsp. baking soda

¼ tsp. salt

⅓ c. milk

1 egg white

5.3 oz blueberry yogurt

1 c. whole blueberries

Combine oats, flour, brown sugar, baking soda, and salt together in medium bowl.

Add milk and egg white, mixing and combining until moist but thick.

Press half of crust mixture into the bottom of a greased 9-inch by 9-inch pan.

Spread yogurt over crust, then sprinkle blueberries evenly on top of yogurt.

Gently sprinkle remaining crust mixture on top.

Bake at 350 degrees for 20-25 minutes. Let cool 1 hour before cutting.

NOTE: substitute other flavors of yogurt and other fresh fruit to customize flavor (i.e., strawberry yogurt with fresh strawberries, peach-mango yogurt with diced peaches)

Serves 9.

V's Texas-Style Potatoes

2 packages frozen shredded hash brown potatoes

½ c. melted butter, plus ¼ c. melted butter, divided

1 tsp. salt

¼ tsp. pepper

½ c. diced onion

1 can cream of chicken soup, undiluted

2 c. shredded cheddar cheese

12 oz. sour cream

1 c. corn flake cereal

Thaw hash browns in refrigerator overnight.

Dice onion.

In a separate large dish, melt ½ c. butter and add salt and pepper.

Combine onion, butter mixture, sour cream, and cream of chicken soup.

Add in potatoes and cheese and stir to coat.

Top with corn flakes and ¼ c. melted butter.

Bake at 350 degrees for 45 minutes. Let sit for 5-10 minutes before serving.

NOTE: Consider substituting cream of mushroom or cream of celery soup for cream of chicken. If desired, add shredded cooked chicken to create a heartier casserole.

Serves 12.

Lemon Cake Pops

1 white cake, prepared and unfrosted

8 oz. cream cheese, room temperature

2 sticks butter, softened

1 tsp. vanilla extract

2 tsp. lemon extract

3 ½ c. powdered sugar

1 package Wilton candy melts, yellow

Cream together cream cheese, butter, vanilla extract, and lemon extract until fluffy and whipped.

Slowly beat in powdered sugar until creamy.

In separate bowl, crumble cake into fine pieces.

Stir in frosting until a thick dough forms, adding more until balls can be formed. There may be frosting left over. Insert lollipop sticks (or skip, if serving as cake balls). Chill for 30 minutes.

Melt candy melts, then dip cake balls into yellow chocolate coating. Sprinkle with sprinkles before coating hardens, if desired.

NOTE: adding 1 tsp. coconut oil may help thin candy melts until they reach a dippable consistency.

Cotton Candy Cocktails

1 oz vanilla vodka

6 oz lemon lime or club soda

½ c. cotton candy

Place cotton candy in champagne flute.

Top with vodka, then fill with lemon lime or club soda.

NOTE: to prepare Jade-style, add two shots vodka instead of one. To virginize, omit vodka and add additional soda. Consider swapping vanilla vodka for a fruit-flavored vodka or substitute any clear soda to adjust sweetness. Cotton candy will melt when in contact with liquid, so presentation is best when liquids are poured immediately before serving.

Makes 1 cocktail

Raspberry Black Bean Dip

Medium onion, diced

1 can black beans, drained

8 oz. cream cheese

12.5 oz raspberry jalapeno sauce

5 slices pepper jack cheese

Tortilla chips (for dipping)

Layer onions, black beans, cream cheese, jalapeno sauce, and pepper jack cheese in that order in baking dish.

Bake at 350 degrees for 30 minutes or until cheese is melted and dip is hot and bubbly.

Serve with tortilla chips.

Pollo Magnifico

3 chicken breasts, cooked and shredded

8 tortillas (burrito-sized)

16 oz. cream cheese

16 oz. Mexican-blend cheese

Jalapeno, seeded and finely diced

1 packet taco seasoning

Tomato and lettuce (for garnish)

Combine shredded chicken and jalapenos.

Mix in cream cheese, 8 oz. shredded cheese, and taco seasoning.

Divide filling between tortillas. Fold tortillas envelope-style around filling, then place seam-side down on cookie sheet sprayed with cooking spray. Mist tops of tortillas with cooking spray.

Bake at 350 degrees for 15 minutes. Turn over and bake 15 minutes longer.

If desired, sprinkle tops with remaining cheese.

NOTE: to freeze, omit topping cheese and allow to cool. Freeze in airtight container. Reheat by microwaving for 3 minutes, adding cheese halfway through microwaving if desired.

Serves 8.

Beefy Potato Taco Pie

2 pie crusts (homemade or store bought)

¼ c. butter

1 medium onion, diced

⅓ c. flour

1 can beef broth

½ c. milk

1 pkg. taco seasoning

8 oz. shredded cheddar cheese

1 can diced tomatoes

½ bag frozen corn

1 lb. southern-style hash brown potatoes, frozen

1 lb. ground beef, cooked and drained

Line pie plate with bottom pie crust. Set aside.

In saucepan, melt butter on medium heat and sauté onion until tender.

Add flour, stirring constantly, then add beef broth.

Add milk and allow mixture to thicken, stirring occasionally.

Add taco seasoning, then stir in cheese until completely melted.

Coat tomatoes, corn, hash browns, and beef in cheese sauce, then spoon into pie crust.

Place top crust on pie, seal, and cut vents in crust.

Bake at 450 degrees for 30 minutes or until crust is golden and filling is hot and bubbly. Add foil to crust edges if it begins to get too dark.

Cool 15 minutes before cutting and serving.

NOTE: freshly grating cheese from a block, rather than buying pre-shredded cheese, will result in a creamier filling.

Serves 6.

Blended Frozen Strawberry Margaritas

1 lb. strawberries, sliced and destemmed

Juice of 4 limes

12 oz. sweet and sour margarita mix

12 oz. tequila

6 oz. triple sec

6 cups crushed ice

Place all ingredients in blender and blend until a slushy consistency.

Pour into chilled glasses rimmed with coarse sugar and salt.

NOTE: to virginize, omit tequila, substitute non-alcoholic triple sec, and add one more cup ice.

Serves 4.

Chicken Spaghetti

4 chicken breasts

1 chicken bouillon cube

1 lb. spaghetti, broken in half

2 cans cream of mushroom soup

2½ c. grated sharp cheddar cheese

¼ c. diced green bell pepper

¼ c. diced red bell pepper

1 medium onion, diced

1 tsp. seasoned salt

Dash of pepper

Preheat oven to 350 degrees.

Cook chicken in pot with water and bouillon cube until done, then remove chicken and all but two cups of broth. Shred chicken.

Add spaghetti noodles to chicken broth, adding water as needed to cook noodles.

Mix all ingredients except pasta in a casserole dish until well-combined, reserving ½ c. cheddar for topping later. Stir in spaghetti until pasta is well coated.

Bake at 350 degrees for 20 minutes, then top with remaining cheese. Return to oven for 5 minutes or until cheese is melted.

Serve warm.

Mushroom Noodle Bake

12 oz. cottage cheese

½ c. sour cream

2 eggs

1 can mushroom pieces

1 pkg. egg noodles, cooked

1¼ tsp salt

Italian-seasoned breadcrumbs

Combine ingredients (except breadcrumbs and noodles) in casserole dish, then stir in noodles.

Top with Italian-seasoned breadcrumbs.

Bake at 350 degrees for 25 minutes until hot and bubbly.

Not-Quite-Homemade Lemon Sponge Cake

1 box lemon cake mix

3 eggs, separated

⅓ c. oil

1¼ c. water

Beat egg whites to stiff peaks and set aside.

Sift boxed cake mix twice.

Combine cake mix, oil, and water until combined, then gently fold in egg whites.

Place mixture into greased Bundt pan.

Bake at 325 degrees for the length of baking time indicated on the cake mix box, adding additional time as needed until cake tests done.

NOTE: experiment with other flavors of boxed cake mix. Orange, chocolate, and vanilla work particularly well. To make a lemon glaze, add teaspoons of lemon juice to 2 c. powdered sugar until a thin glaze forms and brush over cooled cake.

Lemon White-Chocolate Cookie Bars

1 pkg. white chocolate chip refrigerated cookie dough, thawed

1 c. powdered sugar

8 oz. cream cheese

8 oz. whipped topping, divided

1 small box white chocolate pudding mix

1 small box lemon pudding mix

3 c. cold milk

Lemon zest

Press cookie dough into bottom of greased 9-inch by 13-inch pan.

Bake according to package directions until crust is golden brown. Cool completely.

Mix cream cheese, 1 c. whipped topping, and powdered sugar in medium bowl until combined. Spread over cooled crust.

Combine pudding mixes and cold milk until pudding reaches proper consistency. Spread over cream cheese layer.

Spread remaining whipped topping over pudding mixture, then zest lemon over the top.

Chill for 10 minutes or until ready to serve.

NOTE: experiment with other pudding and cookie flavors. Peanut butter cookie dough works well with 2 boxes chocolate pudding and grated chocolate, white chocolate cookie dough works well with fruit flavored puddings and fresh fruit topping, sugar cookie dough pairs nicely with vanilla pudding, and refrigerated brownie dough works well with white chocolate pudding for a decadent, easy dessert.

Strawberry Pretzel Salad

For the crust:

3/4 c. melted butter

3 tbsp. granulated sugar

2 c. crushed pretzels

Mix ingredients together and spread into a greased 9-inch by 13-inch pan.

Bake at 350 degrees for 8 minutes.

Let cool completely.

For the filling:

8 oz. cream cheese

1 c. granulated sugar

8 oz. whipped topping

Cream together cream cheese and sugar until well-combined.

Fold in whipped topping.

Spread over cooled crust and refrigerate.

For the gelatin layer:

2 c. boiling water

1 pkg. strawberry gelatin

20 oz. frozen sliced strawberries

Mix gelatin into boiling water until dissolved.

Add frozen strawberries and stir.

When gelatin mixture is cool to the touch, but not fully set, carefully pour over cream cheese layer. Refrigerate several hours until gelatin is firm.

Slice and serve.

Strawberry Peach Pie

2 pie crusts (homemade or store bought)
1 c. sugar plus 2 tsp. sugar, divided
⅓ c. all-purpose flour
1 tbsp. corn starch
1 tsp. salt
¼ tsp. cinnamon
⅛ tsp. nutmeg
4 c. sliced fresh peaches
2 c. sliced fresh strawberries
2 tsp. lemon juice
2 tbsp. blanched almonds, optional
Milk, enough to brush over crust

Prepare pie plate with bottom crust. Set aside.

In a large bowl, combine 1 c. sugar, flour, cinnamon, nutmeg, corn starch, and salt.

Stir in peaches and strawberries. Add lemon juice and toss. Set aside for fifteen minutes.

Spoon filling into prepared pie crust, avoiding excess liquid from fruit. Top with second crust.

Brush top crust lightly with milk and top with almonds (optional) and sugar.

Bake at 375 degrees for 30-45 minutes, adding foil on edges of crust if it begins to darken too quickly.

Cool for 1 hour before slicing and serving.

Serves 6.

Honey Honey Punch

½ c. locally sourced honey

½ c. boiling water

¼ c. lemon juice

1 can apricot nectar

1 can pineapple juice

1 c. vodka

10 oz. sparkling apple juice

Fresh lemon slices

Make honey simple syrup by boiling honey and water until honey is dissolved. Let cool.

Pour honey mixture into pitcher. Mix with lemon juice, apricot nectar, pineapple juice, and vodka. Stir.

Carefully mix in sparkling apple juice.

Garnish with fresh lemon slices.

Serve over ice.

Serves 5.

NOTE: to virginize, omit vodka and add additional sparkling apple juice. To make Jade-style, increase vodka to 1.5 c.

Ceremony at Sunset Cocktail

2 oz. tequila

2 oz. pineapple juice

2 oz. bottled strawberry lemonade

1 oz. grenadine

1 c. ice

Maraschino cherries with stems and mandarin orange slices, for garnish

Pour strawberry lemonade in glass. Top with ice. Pour tequila and pineapple juice over ice.

Tilt glass and carefully pour grenadine down the side, allowing it to settle and make layers.

Garnish with cherry and slice of orange.

NOTE: substitute coconut rum or mango rum for a tropical twist. To virginize, omit tequila and add splash of club soda or lemon-lime soda. To make Jade-style, reduce pineapple juice and strawberry lemonade to 1.5 oz each.

Makes 1 cocktail.

Acknowledgements

When I first found out that there was plenty of content online for my favorite ship, I told myself I would look respectfully, but I knew I'd never be fully invested in that world. Within a week, I had not only created an account, but posted my very first fanfiction. Every comment, every like, every reblog, every click of the "kudos" button on Ao3, helped me realize that writing was important to me, not just as a hobby, but as a huge part of my life. While it's taken me a lot of work and editing and growth to get from fanfiction to published author, all these stories have roots in the person I was then, a few years ago. To everyone who read, supported, and championed my work during that time, thank you.

To my family, thank you for the support. Thanks especially to my grandmother, Myria, who asked me every single time we talked on the phone when the next book would be coming, even when I was still only outlining it. That kept driving me forward.

Aunt Lisa, thank you for your texts championing my writing (and for not telling my mom what was under the sticky notes covering the smutty scenes).

To the other part of my soul, the dude I talk to everyday who loves knives and tall skinny masc twinks, I love you. Thanks for the endless conversations, the late nights, and the tears shed as we kill off our favorite OCs and save our more-favorite ones from peril again and again. Thanks especially for being so candid with your thoughts about Jade and about Alex.

Shaneen, Esi Şirin Ay, thank you both for your valuable beta reading that helped tell me I was headed in the right direction. Kris, thanks to you especially for the prompt about Alex's cold; without that, I'd still be wondering how to start the fire.

And thanks especially to everyone who bought and shared *This Christmas*, requested it from your local libraries, and shared your passion for these characters. Without you, there'd be no sequel. Thank you to BJ, who gave me wonderful feedback and helped make the first book a reality, and to Elizabeth, for picking up the torch from there. And thank you to Raevyn, Natasha, and everyone at NineStar Press for the love, support, and effort into book one.

About J.R. Hart

J R Hart is a queer thirtysomething novelist passionate about telling romantic and erotic stories about LGBT+ characters. When J R isn't writing, you can find her at the science museum with her son, cheering for her favorite soccer team, or at The Bean Coffee Co plotting her next work. You can find her on Twitter and Instagram as @jrhartauthor, or on her website at jrhartauthor.com.

Email
jrhartauthor@gmail.com

Twitter
@jrhartauthor

Instagram
@jrhartauthor

Website
www.jrhartauthor.com

Other NineStar books by this author

This Love series

This Christmas

Splash

Also from NineStar Press

I Do (Not) by Anni Lee

Jacob Conner is never getting married.

Not now, not "someday," and certainly not when he's black-out drunk at his sister's wedding in Las Vegas. The whole "waking up in an unfamiliar hotel room with a ring on his finger" thing was probably just a coincidence. Definitely.

He doesn't have much time to dwell on it anyway, as Aaron Craig, his boss, assigns him to be the glorified baby sitter for his older brother for the week. Trevor Craig is as obnoxious as he is handsome, immediately pushing all of Jacob's buttons and all of his boundaries. With one brother trying his patience, and the other acting unusually friendly, Jacob's starting to wonder if he's going to survive his work life long enough to find who put that ring on his finger.

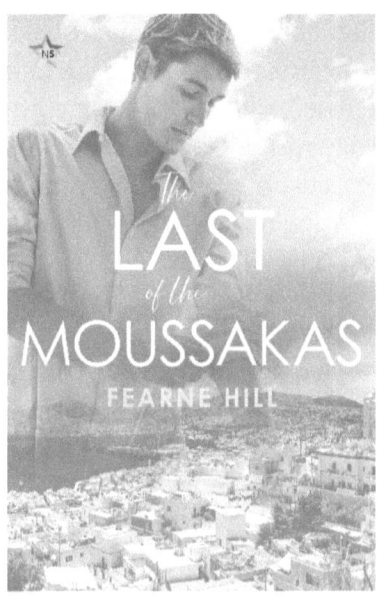

The Last of the Moussakas by Fearne Hill

Max Bergmann is Europe's hottest drum and bass DJ. From the outside, his life is a whirl of glamorous vodka-fueled parties and casual hook-ups, whilst inside he craves the one thing he can't have – his Greek childhood friend, Georgios Manolas.

Following a disastrous PR stunt and one drunken hook-up too many, Max realises the time has come to reassess his life choices. Returning to his childhood home on the Greek island of Aegina, if he wants any chance of having Georgios permanently in his life, he has to delve into the mystery of the longstanding hatred of the Bergmann's by Georgios's family.

Georgios is a chef and has spent his whole life on the tiny Greek island of Aegina. He has held the family restaurant together since he left school, with very little reward, and dreams of one day running a restaurant of his own on the island. Yet if he acknowledges his feelings for Max, he runs the risk of losing not just his traditional Greek family but also his livelihood.

As Max slowly uncovers the secrets of the past, he is left wondering whether a little Greek girl's heart-breaking wartime diary could not only hold the key to his family's history, but could it also unlock his and Georgios's future together?

The Last of the Moussakas is a light-hearted, warm romance about two men's quest for the truth about the past and unlocking a path to a future together.

The Q by Rick R. Reed

Step out for a Saturday night at *The Q*—the small town gay bar in Appalachia where the locals congregate. Whose secret love is revealed? What long-term relationship comes to a crossroad? What revelations come to light? The DJ mixes a soundtrack to inspire dancing, drinking, singing, and falling in (or out) of love.

This pivotal Saturday night at *The Q* is one its regulars will never forget. Lives irrevocably change. Laugh, shed a tear, and root for folks you'll come to love and remember long after the last page.

Connect with NineStar Press

www.ninestarpress.com

www.facebook.com/ninestarpress

www.facebook.com/groups/NineStarNiche

www.twitter.com/ninestarpress

www.instagram.com/ninestarpress